That Dating Thing

by

Mackenzie Crowne

That Dating Thing

Cover Art by *R.J. Morris*

The Wild Rose Press, Inc.
PO Box 708
Adams Basin, NY 14410-0708
Visit us at www.thewildrosepress.com

Publishing History
First Champagne Rose Edition, 2014
Digital ISBN 978-1-62830-014-7
Print ISBN 978-1-62830-418-3

Published in the United States of America

"This dating thing?"

"Or whatever it is you're after," she repeated. As he closed the distance, she stepped back and bumped up against the shark cage. She slapped her spread fingers against his chest to prevent him from coming any closer. "I'm not in the market for a relationship right now."

"Then we don't have a problem, because neither am I." He brushed a fingertip over the perfect skin of her cheekbone. "So, here's what I suggest."

Her eyelids fluttered, pupils dilating, and reluctant temptation replaced the wariness in her dark orbs. Still, she kept a defensive hand on his chest.

"If you insist on negotiating when I've already explained my concerns," she said, holding his gaze, "I'd rather you didn't touch me."

He checked the urge to kiss her at the artless admission of finding his touch disturbing. Instead, he moved his hand to the cage beside her head. He wrapped his fingers around the metal bar and dipped his head, bringing his face closer to hers. She blinked but held her ground, boldly meeting his gaze.

Praise for Mackenzie Crowne

"*THAT DATING THING* is a sweet and sexy contemporary romance that will leave your face frozen with a smile and your stomach churning with happiness by the time you are through with it."

~Sizzling Hot Book Reviews

~*~

"*THAT DATING THING* is a fun romance, with some good conflict to make things interesting."

~Storm Goddess Book Reviews & More

~*~

"I enjoyed every morsel of this story like one would a warm chocolate chip cookie."

~Vonnie Davis, "Romance Writer"

~*~

"I think any romance lover would enjoy this story. It's fun and sweet and all around enjoyable."

~Books Etc.

Dedication

For my men,
Phil, Jared and Kevin,
who suffer through burnt meals, dirty laundry,
and blank looks as I visit with the voices in my head.
For my clan, who always support,
and my girls,
who sit on the deck and listen
to what the voices have to say.

Chapter One

"You look like you've been hit by a truck."

A wince followed Elliott's bark of laughter and scored a direct hit to Rylee's guilt. Considering a truck *had* hit him, she didn't see how he could laugh. She would have nightmares for a year.

"Sorry, big guy. I'm feeling guilty. That always pushes my smartass button."

"I just broke a foot, Rylee."

"A broken foot, concussion, bruised ribs and jaw, and a black eye." Rylee ticked off the offences on her fingers. "And my fault. I know better than to lose concentration in the middle of a group lesson."

"It's hard to concentrate when you're in shock." He grimaced. "We could have picked a better time and place to tell you."

True. The last thing Rylee expected when Sil and Elliott had rushed up to her was to learn they just got married. In the ensuing celebration, she forgot all about the multiple leashes she juggled. No small wonder she hadn't lost control of all four dogs instead of just the one.

"You're right." She narrowed her eyes in accusation. "I don't know why I put up with either of you."

He chuckled in response and a smile teased her mouth.

Her gaze roamed over him, from the crisscross of snaps and buckles that formed the ugly black boot covering his broken foot, up his long legs, to his solid chest and wide shoulders. Regulation length, silver-gray hair capped his wide forehead over intelligent, bright blue eyes. One of those eyes was nearly swollen shut. The blade of his nose sported a wicked scrape and the right side of his face, down to his jaw, was twice its usual size.

In spite of the injuries, the military bearing that carried Colonel Elliott Reed through four decades as "one of the few and the proud" was evident. The man knew how to fill out a T-shirt, and his muscled arms looked as if they could chop through a cord of wood in record time. At sixty, he was still an impressive sight. Rylee understood why Sil blushed like a teenager ever since the colonel moved into River View condominiums six months earlier.

"It was an accident, Rylee." Elliott attempted a roguish waggle of his thick brows, the affectation comically off-kilter due to the swelling. "Besides, having two beautiful women dote on me for the next couple of weeks is well worth a little discomfort."

Rylee grinned. "You say that now. We'll talk again in a couple of days. I've experienced your bride's bedside manner."

"A tough nurse, huh?"

"Does the name *Ratchet* ring any bells?"

His smile was smug, but so was Rylee's. He'd learn the truth soon enough.

The door buzzer sounded and she spun on her heel. "Speak of the devil. She must have forgotten her key again. Brace yourself."

Rylee laughed over her shoulder, passing into the foyer to open the door. The laugh froze on her lips and she blinked, swallowing an audible purr of feminine appreciation. The grainy newspaper photos of Elliott's son had not done him justice.

All spit and polish, his conservative business suit didn't disguise the powerful body it covered. Filling the doorway, those shoulders would look right at home encased in a numbered jersey, bumping up against other mountains of muscle huddled on a fifty-yard line. The face, however, belonged on one of Manhattan's mega-billboards. Combined with the slash of sharp cheekbones, crisply cut lips, linear nose, square jaw, and piercing blue eyes, his short-cropped mane of thick, black hair was overkill. Cologne sales would soar.

He darted his eyes to the plaque on the door, as though double-checking the number, before snapping them back to Rylee. "I'm looking for my father, Colonel Reed."

It's about time.

Rylee bit back her retort before the words could escape. Sil claimed conflicts existed between father and son, long-term conflicts for which Elliott accepted full responsibility. Rylee, of all people, understood the concept of an imperfect parent, but geez. Even after everything he did to destroy her life and the lives of so many others, if a truck hit *her* father she wouldn't wait three days to find out if he was okay.

Cooper Reed may be a seriously gorgeous, younger version of the colonel, but despite having never met him, his slow response alone dropped him three full points on her one-to-ten guy scale. One point for each day he hadn't shown up. Staring up at him, she figured that put him at a solid…hmmm. How was she supposed to calculate when the starting point was off the chart?

You are so shallow, Rylee. Oh, come on. Look at him!

"Is the colonel here, Miss …?"

"Rylee," she chirped, ripped from her musings. "I mean Pierce." She bit the tip of her tongue to keep from rolling her eyes. "I'm Rylee Pierce," she managed finally. "Your father is in the living room."

She left the doorway for him to follow, moving beyond the foyer into Elliott's living room. Similar to her first floor unit, the entire back wall of the condo held windows that framed a panoramic view of Manhattan's skyline across the river. As always, the sight brought a surge of pleasure. This view was the reason she chose River View, the smallest of the three buildings her grandmother left her, as her home. Elliott made his home here for the same reason.

Stretched out on the dark leather couch, Elliott turned his head at their approach. Delight warred with wariness when he spotted his son.

"Coop!" he called out. "I wasn't expecting you, son."

Rylee studied Coop's reaction to his father, searching for the same delight on his handsome face. Instead, his eyes filled with alarm.

"What the hell happened to you?" He skirted the couch for a closer look.

"It's nothing." Elliott flicked a hand, dismissing the obvious wreckage to his face and body. "I had a little accident."

"Don't give me your tough-guy marine crap, Dad." Coop crossed his arms and lifted a challenging brow.

"You look like shit."

Elliott winced and Rylee moved between them. "Keep your voice down," she warned softly. "Can't you see his head is hurting?"

Coop slid his gaze down her body, completing a slow survey on the way back up. A derisive snort flared his nostrils. He turned away, his lips twisting in a smirk, to eye Elliott with mocking regard.

"Progressed to robbing the cradle now, Colonel?"

"Excuse me?" Rylee gasped, forgetting Elliott's hurting head.

He couldn't mean what he was implying. The colonel was old enough to be her father, for heaven's sake, *and* he just married her aunt!

"Cooper," Elliott barked. He briefly squeezed his eyes shut, his voice much softer when he continued. "I know you feel justified in making that assumption, considering my behavior over the years, but you couldn't be more wrong. Rylee is a friend."

Apparently, Cooper Reed meant *exactly* what he implied. She ticked off several more points…down to a solid four.

Straightening to her full five-foot-eight, she pinned him with a derisive stare. Elliott may excuse Coop's assumption, an assumption resulting from those long-term conflicts, but Rylee wasn't of the same mind. His insinuation wasn't just ridiculous, it was insulting. As the only child of the infamous Peter Morris, she grew up fielding far worse. But in her experience, letting insults go unanswered left a person in the weaker position. She far preferred fighting fire with fire.

"A friend whose help wouldn't have been necessary if Elliott's *family*," she aimed an accusatory finger at his chest, "hadn't been too *busy* to bother with him until three days later."

"Rylee," Elliott spoke into the heated silence. "It's not Coop's fault. He didn't know I was hurt."

She dragged her gaze from the confrontational glitter in Coop's eyes back to Elliott. "You said you called him from the hospital and left a message."

"I did. However, I didn't give him any details. I just asked him to call me back."

"Which I have." Coop shot her a dismissive glance before focusing on his father. "Several times. I was out of town on business until this morning. Since you haven't returned any of my half-dozen calls, I came straight from the airport."

"Sorry, son. My phone is probably still in the bag I brought home from the hospital. I've been a little out of sorts."

"You still haven't answered my question." Coop lifted a brow. "What happened?"

"It's my fault," Rylee interrupted.

Two pairs of identical bright blue eyes pinned her like laser beams. She lifted her chin. The jury was still out on whether or not he was a jerk, but Elliott's son wasn't guilty of ignoring his father's accident as she originally thought. Judging a situation without having all the facts was something people consistently did with her and she hated it. Yet she accused him of not caring when just the opposite seemed true. Guilt demanded she apologize.

"I told you, Rylee—"

"Zip it, big guy." She faced Coop. "I owe you an apology. I had you pegged as an uncaring bastard. Since that appears untrue, all I can say is…my bad."

She shrugged. "I've been a little out of sorts myself lately and feeling guilty. Your dad tried to help me and ended up stepping in front of a delivery truck in the process."

"You were hit by a truck?" Coop jerked his head in Elliott's direction, eyebrows jumping nearly to his hairline.

"One of my students broke loose," she added in a rush, drawing his attention back to her. "Your father dashed after Pippin when he ran into the street."

"Pippin?"

"I'm a dog trainer," she explained. "Pippin is one of my students. Unfortunately, he has a nose for trouble." She smiled gratefully at Elliott. "Your father saved his life."

"All this," Coop lifted his chin toward Elliott's swollen, scraped face. "For a dog?"

Major loss of the points he just regained. She frowned.

"He's a cute little guy," Elliott insisted and winked at her.

Rylee couldn't help returning Elliott's grin, rolling her eyes at his ridiculous description of her troublesome student. As with Rylee, Pippin had charmed Elliott, but though the dog was many things, including cute, he wasn't little.

"If you say so," Coop muttered. "So, what's the damage?" He glanced at the boot. "Is the ankle broken?"

"Compound fracture." Rylee ignored Elliott's scowl. Their relationship might be estranged, but Coop obviously knew his father. His tough-guy marine comment was right on the money. Elliott would

7

downplay the damage if she let him. "And a concussion," she continued. "And bruised ribs. His jaw isn't broken, thank God, just badly bruised. He won't be eating solids for a while."

Coop's mouth thinned at the list of injuries. He nodded. "I appreciate your caring for him until I could get here. And I apologize if I insulted you earlier."

"If?" Rylee crossed her arms. Was that his idea of an apology? Huh! His efforts sucked.

"I apologize for insulting you." His amendment seemed sincere until a challenge gleamed in his eyes. "I had you pegged as a gold-digging bimbo. Since that appears to be untrue, all I can say is…my bad."

A startled laugh escaped at having her words tossed back at her.

Points for him.

"Apology accepted." Abandoning her crossed arms, she perched beside Elliott's shoulder on the arm of the couch. "A gold-digging bimbo, huh?" She grinned down at Elliot. "Is it weird I consider that a compliment?" The men's matching, blank stares made her laugh. "So, Coop, Elliott says you work in the D.A.'s office. That must be exciting."

"The constant chaos keeps my interest."

"What type of cases do you handle?"

He would have been in his first years of college during the time her father was the number one focus of the New York City justice system, but considering their sudden familial connection, if Cooper Reed was going to be trouble, she wanted to know.

"I'm in the violent crimes unit."

She suppressed a relieved sigh. Though her father's crimes were big news back then, the only violence had been to his investor's portfolios. "Ah, avenging the victims of the city's dark side. No wonder Elliott is so proud of you."

Surprise flickered in Coop's eyes and he shot a glance at Elliott before shrugging. "I'm not quite as quixotic as you make me sound. My job is to see that the guilty pay."

"You may consider that just a job, but I am always impressed by people who take on tough tasks for no other reason than they need doing."

He stared at her, a slight frown creasing his brow.

"He doesn't do well with compliments, does he?" she asked Elliott.

He grinned. "He's not sure what to make of you."

"He's not alone." She laughed. "I'm not sure what to make of *myself* most of the time." She slapped her thighs and stood. "I was just going to bring your father his lunch." She smiled at Coop. "Soup. There's plenty, if you'd like to join him."

"Uh."

She turned on her heel before he could form a reply. "Two bowls coming up."

Chapter Two

Coop followed Rylee's progress across the room toward the open kitchen area. The swish of her ponytail, a long, straight, swath of jet-black hair, drew his attention down to the lazy swing of her hips wrapped in faded denim. A walk like hers should be against the law, but any man with eyes would risk a felony charge for the chance to appreciate the view.

Plenty to appreciate about the rest of her, as well. Half a foot shorter than his six-two, she was all legs and a slim body, with an enticing fullness where a man likes to see curves. Her plain, white tank top displayed a couple of those curves to perfection, as well as the toned smoothness of her tanned arms and shoulders.

Her facial features were delicate, with high cheekbones and a wide mouth. The black hair, dark-chocolate eyes and lightly bronzed skin indicated the presence of at least some Native American blood. One of the southern tribes possibly, considering the melodic drawl softening the bite of her East Coast accent. The same bite that sharpened when she warned him to keep his voice down, and turned downright slicing after his spiteful insinuation.

Truth be told, he wouldn't have been surprised to learn his insinuation was dead on the mark, despite the obvious age difference. His father always did have an eye for the ladies and wouldn't have missed a woman who looked like Rylee Pierce. Add to that her generous personality, evidenced by her willingness to help a friend in need, and her sweet, if quirky, sense of humor, and… Hell, no mystery why he was relieved at their mutual denial of a personal relationship.

At the far end of the condo she moved about Elliott's kitchen with familiarity, assembling items and stirring a big pot on the stove. The distance made her overhearing improbable, but he kept his voice low just the same.

"She's…" He ran his tongue over his teeth, searching for the right words to describe the woman working to serve them up lunch. He turned back to Elliott, settling on, "something else."

"You have no idea."

"Who is she?" Coop asked, dropping into the chair across from the couch.

"She owns River View. Her condo is below mine."

"Owns the building?" Coop's gaze flicked to the kitchen where she ladled soup into bowls with easy grace. "A dog trainer who owns a prime piece of riverfront? I wasted my money on law school."

Elliott chuckled. "From what I understand, she inherited the building from her grandmother."

Coop grunted and settled down to the matter at hand. "Give me a list of what you need. I'll pack you a bag."

"Where am I going?"

"My place. I don't have any traveling on the docket for the next couple of weeks, so I'll be home at night. I'll hire someone in to stay with you during the day."

Elliott shook his head. "Not necessary, though I appreciate the offer."

"Recuperating at my place is the most logical solution, Dad. I have a full caseload right now. I need to be in the city, close to the office and court. Adding commute time to twelve hour days will cut into the time I can be around."

"I don't need you to stay with me, here or at your place."

"Dad." Coop sighed. "You're going to need assistance, at least for the next few days."

"I have it covered."

Coop frowned. Whenever Elliott Reed used that tone, the topic was closed for further discussion. "At least let me hire a nurse. I'll feel better knowing someone is with you."

"You'd just be wasting your money."

Rylee strolled toward them, a tolerant smile curving her lips. A dishtowel lay draped over one shoulder while wisps of fragrant steam curled from the matching bowls on the tray she carried.

"Sil will just find a reason to send your nurse packing." She set the tray on the coffee table. "She's territorial."

She handed the towel to Elliott, and then picked up one of the bowls. Cocking her head, she studied him. "Do you need help? Or can you feed yourself?"

Elliott grinned. "I can manage, but I wouldn't dare hurt your feelings if you insist on feeding me."

She straightened, handing him the bowl and a spoon. "Save the charm for Sil, big guy. You'll need it." She turned to Coop.

"I've been feeding myself for years," he said dryly.

Delighted laughter filled the room and a dimple winked in her cheek. She held out the second bowl. "A man of hidden talents."

His gut muscles tightened at the humor dancing in her dark eyes, and because he always believed in exploring innate, physical signals of attraction, he let his fingers linger against hers a bit longer than necessary as he took the bowl. Her eyes widened at the deliberate contact, her pupils dilating owlishly, and the tightening in his gut intensified.

Interesting…and unexpected, considering Rylee Pierce wasn't his usual type. Long, cool blondes were his preference.

Like Ashley? A spurt of irritation had him clenching his jaw. That relationship was over. A woman who considered attending a fashion show more important than putting a murderer behind bars wasn't worth the effort, no matter how good the sex.

"Who's Sil?" he asked, covering his irritation by scooping up a spoonful of soup. His taste buds cheered at the savory bite of excellent pasta fagioli.

"Who's Sil?" Rylee repeated and blinked. Coop followed her confused glance, darting in Elliott's direction. His father studiously filled his mouth with soup as though starved. "Silvia Burke" Rylee said slowly, "is my aunt." She turned to Coop. "She's running an errand. She'll be back soon."

"Is she his nurse?"

Elliott choked on his soup.

Sudden tension hardened Rylee's delicate facial features. She moved behind the arm of the couch, her mouth pinched flat in annoyance. Coop flinched when she landed two healthy thumps between Elliott's shoulder blades with the flat of her hand. He was about to point out that thumping someone with bruised ribs was a bad idea, when the slam of the condo's front door stopped him.

The woman who stepped into the room looked like a cross between an Irish gypsy and a hippy. Faded bellbottom jeans, frayed at the cuffs, rested on neon-pink toenails that peeked out from a pair of chunky, leather sandals. Her wispy, floral-print peasant blouse floated about her hips and displayed some impressive curves. A silk scarf wrapped around her head of short, chestnut hair. Large, silver hoops adorned her ears and matched the collection of bangles circling one slim wrist. Her pale skin was close to flawless and the sparkle in her green eyes enhanced the illusion of ageless perfection.

The mysterious Aunt Sil?

Crossing the room, she changed direction mid-stride. "You must be Cooper."

No Northeastern bite here. Mint juleps and hoopskirts echoed in her pure, southern drawl. Coop rose to his feet when she stopped before him.

"I'm Silvia." Her steady, green gaze roamed his face. "The people I care about call me Sil. It's a pleasure to finally meet you, Cooper."

To his surprise, instead of offering him her hand, she rose on her chunky sandals and planted a smacking kiss on his mouth. Before he could respond, she spun toward Elliott, dropped a paper bag from a local pharmacy on the coffee table and settled on the couch at his hip. The bangles at her wrist jangled as she brushed gentle fingertips over his swollen jaw.

"Damn, sugar. He looks just like you. I can't decide which of you is yummier."

Coop didn't need the familiar itch at the back of his

neck to tell him Silvia Burke was the latest in Colonel Elliott Reed's babe parade. Reclaiming his seat, Coop glanced between his father and Rylee's aunt, making eyes at each other like a couple of giddy teenagers.

Rylee's tension suddenly made sense. She didn't understand, or appreciate, Elliott's reluctance to mention his true relationship with her aunt. Coop could have explained the oversight had nothing to do with Silvia. He and Elliott simply didn't discuss the colonel's lady-friends. The purposeful omission helped keep the peace.

Elliott's smile, when he met Coop's gaze across the coffee table, resembled a guilty grimace. Coop shook his head.

"How are you feeling, sugar?" Sil murmured.

"Better." Elliott's smile softened when he refocused on Silvia. "Now that you're back."

She laughed low in her throat. "Aren't you the charmer? I picked up your medicine."

"You're all the medicine I need."

Coop glanced at Rylee, standing off to the side. The tension was still evident, but her lips were curved indulgently, as if to say, *what are you gonna do?* She rolled her eyes and mimicked sticking her index finger down her throat. When his brows rose in response, her smile morphed into a grin.

"Ahem." She cleared her throat and drew the lovebirds' attention. "I'd tell the two of you to get a room, but I'd be wasting my time. Now that you're back, Sil, I need to get downstairs before Pippin organizes a revolt."

"He's still here?" she demanded. "I thought you said you were flunking him out of the program."

Rylee shrugged helplessly. "I sat him down to explain why he needed to go and he got me with his 'don't you believe in me anymore?' look. I caved."

"He's playing you, Rylee," Sil admonished with an arch of her brow.

"I know."

"Do you want me to take over? He has your number."

"No, this is between the two of us. And after what happened to Elliott, it's personal. I'll handle him."

"You're scaring Coop, ladies," Elliott snickered and all three looked Coop's way.

Damned straight they were scaring him. Conversing with dogs? Either Rylee Pierce and her gypsy-hippy aunt were a couple of nut cases or they believed they were some kind of dog whisperers. He wasn't sure which was worse.

"Sil and I run The Canine Academy." Rylee explained. "A kind of boot camp for troubled dogs. Close communication between handler and animal is essential to the program's success."

Not having a clue what to say, Coop grunted and she grinned.

"Sounds crazy, I know, but the proof is in the pudding or in this case the pedigree. We retrain dogs and their owners who have had no luck elsewhere. Sort of a last ditch appeal, as with Pippin. And speaking of which, I'm out of here."

She bent over Elliot, kissing him on his bruised cheek. The movement displayed her sweetly curved, denim-covered ass like a visual gift, snagging Coop's appreciative gaze. She straightened far too quickly for his liking.

"I'll be back later." Her promise sounded more like a warning to Coop's ears. "Nice meeting you, Coop," she said, turning a smile on him.

"Same here." He rose, glancing at his watch. "I'll head down with you. I have to get back to the office." He eyed Elliott. "I'll be checking in. You have my number if you need anything."

Elliott nodded.

"I'll take care of your daddy," Sil promised, then lowered her tone to more of a demand than invitation. "You come back soon, Cooper Reed. Now that I've met you, I'm just *dying* with curiosity. I'll feed you and grill you on every little detail of your life."

A smile twitched his lips and he shook his head at her unapologetic audacity. He pointed at the empty bowls on the coffee table. "Was the soup your creation or your niece's?"

"Rylee was the chef today, but I did teach her everything she knows."

"Then I'll be back."

"A charmer," she drawled. "Just like your daddy."

Coop followed Rylee out of the condo and across the balcony circling the second floor of the building. The reconfigured two-story warehouse consisted of six luxury condos, three on each floor, forming a U. The center-front of the building contained a charming, park-like courtyard. With stunning views of the city at the back and access to the lush common area facing the street, he could understand Elliott's desire to own a unit at River View. What Coop didn't get was how Elliott managed the price tag. But the one time he had asked after the down payment, Elliott answered with a vague, "I shuffled a few things around."

Rylee bypassed the metal-caged elevator at the center of the balcony, heading for one of the two curving stairways leading to the courtyard. She skipped down the steps like a schoolgirl heading to her next class. Coop followed more sedately, his eyes on the seductive roll of her hips. On the ground floor, she stopped at the door below Elliott's and pressed a key into the lock. A distant barking echoed inside.

"Have you got a kennel in there?" Coop stopped by her side.

She opened the door, that intriguing dimple winking in her smile. "Actually, I do."

One of the kennel's occupants drew Coop's attention, appearing from behind the door. The sleek Boxer eyed Coop, its cropped ears flicked forward in interest above watchful, mahogany eyes and a blunt muzzle.

"The infamous Pippin?" Coop guessed.

Rylee widened the opening and scrubbed a hand between the dog's ears. "This is Annabelle, my roommate. Say hello to Coop, Belle."

Belle immediately dropped to her haunches. Coop hesitated, feeling foolish, and then accepted the dog's offered paw. After a single pump, he let go.

"You run the dog thing from your home?"

"Are you asking out of curiosity or as a government official?"

Prickly *and* beautiful…

"I left my government-official hat at the office."

She chuckled. "The building is zoned for business and since it's only Belle and me, I have the room. A separate business entrance is located around back along with a patch of lawn where we work the dogs and their owners."

He nodded. "Can I ask you a question?"

"That depends." The subtle wariness in her eyes didn't quite match the cheekiness of her response. "If you're asking for tips on how to get your puppy to stop eating your briefcases, I'll have to charge you a consultant's fee."

"I'm puppy-less at the moment." He grinned, and then lifted his eyebrows incredulously. "Briefcases?"

"You'd be surprised what dogs find appetizing."

He shook his head in wonder. "No, I don't need any dog advice. I wanted to ask how long my father has been seeing your aunt."

"Five months." When he frowned, she asked, "Why? Is there a problem?"

"Not exactly. I just know the colonel. Your aunt seems like a nice woman. I wouldn't want to see her hurt."

"Why would she be hurt?"

"Six months is about Elliott's limit." His remark sounded harsh, but then the truth often was. "That's about the time he usually walks away."

"I don't think that will be the case this time."

"For your aunt's sake, I hope that's true, but…" He shrugged.

Her gaze darted to the landing above. She said nothing for a long moment, cocking her head to study him as though she was struggling to make up her mind about something. Those dark eyes, so clearly assessing, sent blood racing from his head and upper body to gather below his waist. He drew a slow breath at the pleasant rush of arousal.

"That won't be the case this time," she repeated

with firm resolve.

He cleared his throat. "And you know this because?"

Utter confidence filled her tight smile. "Because…if Elliott even thinks of walking away from Sil, he'll have to deal with *me*."

Chapter Three

"You what?"

"I married her."

Holding the phone to his ear, Coop straightened from the open file on his desk to sprawl back in the chair.

"Did you hear me?"

"I heard you, Dad. I just don't believe you."

"I married Silvia Burke three days ago," Elliott repeated, his voice hard with resolve.

"Okay, I'll bite. Why?"

"Because I'm in love with her."

Coop snorted. "Right. What happens when the next babe comes along and you decide you're in love with her? You have a short attention span with women, but at least you haven't married any of them. Not since…"

"Since your mother?" Elliott finished.

Coop frowned. He rarely thought of the woman who gave birth to him, much less discussed her with his father. Claudia Reed made her choice, walking away without a backward glance, and though Elliott stuck around, doing his best to raise their son, Coop divided the blame for their broken marriage evenly. Whatever other problems were between his parents, Elliott's womanizing played a large part in their breakup.

"My *mother* has little to do with this, but while we're on the subject, that didn't work out very well, did

21

it?"

"Coop." Elliott sighed. "Claudia and I were young and stupid. Selfish too, in our own ways. You and I have never really discussed what happened—"

"And I don't see the need now," Coop interrupted.

"No, I don't suppose you would." Elliott paused. "I'll simply say this. I never remarried after your mother because, although I've loved many of the women I've known over the years, I was never *in* love with them."

"Give me a break, Colonel. You sound like a greeting card."

"You don't exactly live the life of a monk, yourself," Elliott mocked, "so you know what it is to love women. But what you don't know is that when the *right* woman comes along, everything changes."

Coop dropped his head back against the chair and closed his eyes. "I'm not sure what you want me to say, Dad."

"Congratulations would be a good start."

He pinched the bridge of his nose. "Congratulations."

Elliott chuckled at Coop's dry tone. "One last thing. You have your doubts. Nothing I can do about that, but Sil is important to me. I'd like for you to get to know her."

"Dad," Coop started to object. His childhood memories were filled with the faces of women Elliott brought around for Coop to get to know, only so the colonel could move on to the next, right about the time Coop became attached. He hated the familiar, oily nausea those memories produced.

"I married Silvia, Coop," Elliott said as though

reading Coop's mind. "I'm not asking you to welcome her with open arms, just to keep an open mind and give me the chance to prove this time, this woman, is different."

"I'm not a little boy anymore and you don't need my approval."

"But I want your approval, son, and Silvia is innocent in our conflicts. She wants to get to know you. Give her a chance, please. Give *us* a chance."

Unsure if Elliott was referring to the relationship he shared with Silvia, or the one they shared as father and son, Coop remained silent, scraping a hand over his face.

"Sil wanted me to invite you to dinner tomorrow night. Will you come?"

A soft knock on the open office door drew Coop's attention. He opened his eyes and straightened, waving in the familiar blond giant. Tim Watson crossed the room to the seat across from Coop's desk.

"Why not," he said into the phone. "What time?"

"Six."

"Okay."

"Thank you, son," Elliott said quietly.

"I'll see you then." Coop disconnected the call, unconvinced of his father's sincerity, but intrigued all the same.

"Welcome back." Tim's forbidding face, complete with a bulbous nose bearing the signs of a youth spent on the mean streets of Detroit, wore an easy smile. A lawyer by degree, Tim's true gift was his uncanny talent for sniffing out details others often missed. More than two decades with the D.A.'s office and he'd yet to argue a case, a circumstance the entire office found more than acceptable. As head of the investigative department, his fingerprints were on most of the files in the building, contributing to the impressive conviction rate the office enjoyed.

The older man's sleuthing abilities were instrumental in the prosecution of Coop's first case, when the incumbent D.A. took a chance on a decorated marine's son whose bar results were still sticky with wet ink. Coop won the case, and in return, Tim earned Coop's gratitude and respect. Eight years later, Tim and his wife, Lilly, were Coop's closest friends.

"How'd it go?"

A moment passed before Coop realized Tim referred to his Chicago trip to secure extradition of the man responsible for a string of fires resulting in at least two fatalities, and not the bizarre conversation he'd just shared with his father. He picked up a file, leaning forward to hand it across the desk.

"They're willing to extradite unless the victim of his latest fire dies, but the prognosis looks good."

"That's what we wanted to hear." Tim opened the file to skim the top page.

"Yeah."

Tim locked onto Coop's face. "It's good news. So why do you look like you just caught your girlfriend in bed with another man?"

Coop scrubbed a hand over his jaw, bristly with the beginnings of a five-o'clock shadow. "My father was hit by a truck three days ago."

"Damn." Tim straightened in the chair. "Sorry, Coop. Is he okay?"

"Bumps and bruises, concussion and a broken foot. He'll be sore for a while, but it looks like he'll be fine."

"And?" Tim prompted, handing back the file.

Coop set it aside and absently clicked a pen on and off with his thumb. "And he got married."

"The colonel got married?" Surprise made Tim's thick blond brows slam together to form one bushy slash.

"He claims he's in love with her."

Tim shook his head. "Your dad has blown through a lot of women over the years, but he didn't marry any of them. Maybe he is."

Coop grunted, hearing his father's sentiment echoed in his friend's reasoning.

"Who is she? Have you met her?"

"About an hour ago. Her name is Silvia Burke. She runs a dog training service."

"A dog trainer? How did he meet her?"

"Her niece owns his building and lives downstairs. She and Silvia run the dog thing together."

"A dog trainer who owns a building in Long Island City?"

Coop nodded. "That was my exact reaction. Apparently the building was part of an inheritance."

"You want me to check her out? Silvia, I mean, not the niece. Off the books, of course, on my own time."

Conscious of the legal considerations inherent in his position, Coop never broke the rules. In the process of doing his job, Tim often balanced precariously on the blade of justice, but Coop never had reason to doubt his ethics. He wasn't surprised by the private offer.

"I hadn't thought that far." He *had* thought far enough to know he would be checking out the niece through a closer, much more personal inspection. The renewed tightening of his stomach muscles made him smile. "But checking her out might not be a bad idea. Dad may not be loaded by Manhattan standards, especially since buying the condo, but he's not exactly broke."

"What do you know about her?"

"Not much, other than her name. I assume she lives in the area, but you couldn't tell by listening to her. Deep south I'd say, from her Scarlett O'Hara accent."

"A southern belle?"

Coop chuckled, seeing again his father's bride in his mind's eye. He tipped back in his chair. "She's a little hard to describe. Her mode of dress is straight out of the sixties, but I'd put her at closer to forty-five or fifty."

"What about the niece? If I run into trouble, I may have to cross-reference to get a hit."

"Rylee Pierce, mid-to-late twenties. She owns the dog training service. The Canine Academy. You can start there."

"Silvia Burke," Tim repeated. "I've heard that name somewhere." His eyes grew unfocused as he stared into inner space. He snapped his fingers. "Isn't Silvia Burke the administrator of The Adam's House Foundation?"

"The military charity?"

"That's the one. They've been advertising their big Fourth of July fundraiser over on Roosevelt Island."

Coop tapped the pen against the edge of the desk, considering his impression of his father's gypsy wife before sitting forward. "Dad's Silvia runs the dog service with her niece. That must be a different Silvia Burke."

"I'll see what I can find." Tim pushed to his feet.

"The colonel married," he repeated, shaking his head.

****

Rylee let herself inside Elliot's condo, waggling her pointed finger in front of Pippin's nose in the sign for quiet. Beside him, Belle was the picture of patience. The Boxer's serene temperament tended to calm the ten-month-old Great Dane, and for this exercise, Rylee needed all the help she could get. In her opinion, a good portion of Pippin's behavioral problems stemmed from a hypersensitivity to the emotions of his handler. Tension, whether positive or negative, flipped Pippin's switch.

The coming conversation should have him bouncing off the walls.

What were Elliott and Sil up to, and why didn't Elliott want his son to know they were married? The song and dance they performed earlier didn't bode well for Sil's future happiness, especially considering Coop's comments before he left.

Rylee liked Elliott. What's more, she owed him for resurrecting the spark missing in Sil since Adam's death, three days after he'd arrived in Afghanistan, eight years ago. While her cousin's death left a hole in Rylee, losing her son had flattened Sil. Since meeting Elliott, Sil's natural buoyancy had returned. If Elliot hurt her by being less than they believed him to be...

The colonel had some explaining to do.

Which would have to wait. A commercial blared on TV, not quite drowning out the snuffling snores from the man on the couch. Spotting Elliott, Pippin lost focus and started in his direction, but returned to heel at the snap of Rylee's fingers. She was anxious enough to consider stomping over to Elliott herself, to poke him awake and demand some answers. She ignored the urge, continuing into the kitchen where Sil's flour-coated hands wrestled a large ball of dough on the table.

For Pippin, Elliott's presence was a curiosity. Sil's was a temptation he couldn't resist. He paid no attention to Rylee's signal to halt, his large paws scrabbling for purchase on the hardwood floor as he leapt for Sil. Rylee popped his leash. Startled by the unexpected pressure at his neck, he halted then stood quivering. To her satisfaction, he followed Belle's example and dropped to his haunches at her command. She extended her hand, palm down, and both dogs dropped to the floor.

"Good dogs," she praised, showing her palm. "Stay."

"Impressive." Sil eyed Pippin. "He would have been jumping and licking a couple of days ago."

"He's smart, but emotionally motivated, so I'll say this as serenely as possible." Rylee propped her hands on her hips. "What the hell was all of that about earlier? Elliott almost drowned himself in his soup to avoid telling his son you're his wife. What's going on, Sil?"

"Hush," Sil scolded, her eyes darting in Elliott's direction.

"He's out cold." Rylee snorted. "The building could collapse and he wouldn't notice."

"His pain pills have kicked in."

"Uh-huh." Rylee went to the refrigerator. She pulled out a pitcher of sweet tea, setting it on the table with a thump. "And you're not going to distract me by reminding me he's hurt. How could he do that to you, and why would you let him?"

Sil grimaced, resting her hands on the makings of her biscuits. "That's not how it is, Rylee."

"Really? Then explain, because I don't understand."

"Elliott simply wanted to tell Coop about us in private. When he showed up like that, Elliott got a bit flustered and didn't know what to say."

"Didn't know what to say?" Rylee spread her hands. "How about, hey, son, meet your new step-momma?"

At her sharp tone, Pippin whined. Before he could scramble to his feet, Rylee firmly commanded, "Pippin, stay."

The whining increased and indecision shown in his gaze, which snapped back and forth between her and Sil. "Stay," she repeated.

He dropped his head to his paws with a mutinous look.

Rylee turned her arched brows on Sil, who sighed.

"It's complicated."

"Why? I know you said they have issues, but they seemed to get along okay to me. Why would Elliott assume Coop would have a problem learning you'd married?"

"Any problem Coop might have wouldn't be with me, specifically, but with the situation." Silvia grabbed a hand towel to wipe her hands, and then used the damp cloth to cover the ball of biscuit dough. "Coop was just a boy when his mother left. After the divorce…well, Elliott didn't handle things very well. A lot of women came and went out of that little boy's life, Rylee. Being a man and a soldier on the move more often than not, Elliott didn't recognize what the constant upheaval was doing to Cooper. His womanizing caused a rift between them. The relationship is still on the shaky side."

Rylee knew all about father-child conflicts and, in her opinion, holding onto them was a complete waste of energy. She snorted. "So…what? You're going to keep your marriage a secret from him? Because I have to tell you, Sil, that sounds like a badly written sitcom to me. Cooper Reed isn't a little boy anymore. What does Elliott think he'll do when he finds out you're married, throw a temper tantrum?"

Sil grinned. "Nothing so dramatic." She plucked two glasses from the cabinet and brought them to the table for the tea. "From what I understand, discussions between them can sometimes get a little dicey. Elliott, bless his heart, wanted to spare me the experience. He called Coop after you'd both left and explained the situation." She sat down, leaning back in the chair with her glass. "Which is a pure shame, if you ask me. There is nothing I would have enjoyed more than watching two such *fine* looking specimens go toe-to-toe over little old me."

Rylee couldn't help but snicker as she dropped into a chair. That was Sil. Men delighted her, even when they behaved like pre-pubescent idiots. And though Rylee would never admit it, Elliott's and Coop's altercation was something she wouldn't have minded seeing herself. As Sil so bluntly pointed out, the Reed men were yummy.

"So, what was the verdict?" Rylee picked up her glass. "Did the hunky lawyer pitch a fit when he found out his daddy got married?"

"Hunky?" Sil parroted, slapping her fingertips over the shocked little "oh" she formed with her lips. She chuckled when Rylee frowned. "Sugar, it warms my heart that you noticed. You're far too oblivious when it comes to men."

"Not oblivious," Rylee corrected. "Busy."

Rylee's infrequent dating, or more precisely, the reason behind her *disinterest* in dating, was one of her aunt's favorite subjects. When Sil cast a cautious glance in Elliott's direction, Rylee knew they were about to revisit the issue.

"A real man wouldn't give a damn who your daddy is. If you don't bother to look, you won't ever find him."

"What are you talking about? I look. I went on a date three weeks ago."

"You went to *dinner* three weeks ago, and took on two new students the very next day so you'd be too busy to give the man a second opportunity to learn more about you."

"Please." Rylee scowled. "He stared at my boobs the entire meal. On the cab ride home, he actually had the balls to announce he was about to give me the best orgasm of my life. He's lucky I didn't make sure *he* never had another orgasm in *his* life." She shook her head. "What's with guys who consider a steak and a glass of wine foreplay?"

Sil laughed.

"Besides, I let a guy learn more about me once and look how that worked out."

Sil's laugh died on a disgusted frown. "Marcus Perry is a mama's boy and his mama is an overbearing, ignorant bitch."

Rylee agreed with the assessment of her ex-fiancé *and* his mother, but that didn't change the facts. When your father was famous for bilking thousands of people out of billions of dollars, people tended to paint you with the same brush, deserved or not.

"Face it, Sil, once people learn I'm Ponzi Pete's little girl, my innocence doesn't matter. Keeping my true identity a secret from strangers is one thing, but I'm uncomfortable with the idea of developing a relationship with a guy while lying by omission."

Sil reached across the table to cover Rylee's hand. "Just as people are wrong for equating you with your daddy, you are wrong to equate all men with that weasel Marcus."

"Even if that was what I was doing, and I'm not saying it is," Rylee added quickly. "I already feel like a one-armed juggler. Between the dogs and Adam's House, a man is the last thing I need in my life."

"You love the dogs." Sil waved off her argument. "As for Adam's House, Brian could run the Foundation's projects with his eyes closed."

Sil had a point. The dogs were a joy and Brian Hurley was more suited to his chosen work than any man Rylee knew. Not only did Brian have the talent to handle the foundation's projects, he'd loved her cousin Adam like a brother, just as Rylee had. Growing up next door, Brian was Adam's friend long before Rylee came to live with her aunt and cousin, and like them, Brian welcomed Rylee into his life with open arms. To hear Sil tell it, Rylee, Adam, and Brian grew to adulthood exploring the streets of Jackson, Mississippi like the three musketeers.

Life changed with Adam's death, but Brian's friendship eased the grief. And when Rylee suggested he help grow the foundation named for the man they'd all loved, he jumped at the opportunity. Under his guidance, the foundation's projects were flourishing, putting Rylee's unwanted inheritance to good use.

She had been stunned the morning of her twenty-fifth birthday to receive a visit from an attorney representing the estate of Agnes Pierce. Her uber-rich maternal grandmother hadn't approved of Peter Morris, and had cut Rylee's mother out of her life long before Rylee was born. Rylee had never even met the woman, so learning she was the recipient of Agnes's estate was a shock.

She immediately knew she couldn't keep the hefty inheritance. Ponzi Pete's victims would scream bloody murder if they discovered his only child was suddenly worth thirty million. Besides, wealth, or more precisely the pursuit of wealth, had destroyed her family.

Upon receipt of the inheritance, Rylee chose River View, the smallest of the old warehouse buildings included in Agnes' bequest, to make her home. She contracted Brian to do the rehab, with the idea of offering the remaining units to returning vets, in honor of the sacrifice Adam and so many others had made.

River View turned out even better than she envisioned, and the experience was so rewarding she couldn't help thinking *why stop there*? With Brian's assistance, they could turn Agnes' remaining warehouses into affordable housing units for dozens more deserving vets.

Never one to think small, Sil pointed out how others might agree with the sentiment and the concept of The Adam's House Foundation was born.

Figuring out the legalities took some doing, but Rylee's anonymous contribution got things off the ground. Because of her father's notoriety, Rylee kept her name out of foundation business, but no detail escaped her notice, and ultimately, she had the final say when it came to Adam's House's interests. To the world, however, Silvia was the force behind the mission, and Brian Hurly was the muscle.

"Speaking of Brian." Rylee noted the time on her watch. "I've got to go. I'm supposed to meet him in twenty minutes to check out a building he has his eye on."

Having reached the limit of his juvenile attention span, Pippin was up and scrambling across the room the moment Rylee shifted in her chair to rise. He dove for Sil, who laughed and blocked his approach. Once she convinced him to sit properly, she turned a raised brow on Rylee.

"This conversation isn't finished."

Rylee laughed mirthlessly, reaching for Pippin's dangling leash. "It never is."

Sil patted Pippin's head before rising. "You're too precious, inside and out, to let your father's legacy hold you back from building a full life."

"Well, you'll have to keep your fairy-godmother wand on idle for now. I've got work to do."

Rylee called Belle to heel and headed for the living room.

"Oh, I almost forgot," Sil called to her back. "We're expecting you for dinner tomorrow night. A family thing. Brian will be here." She paused before adding in a satisfied drawl, "And the hunky lawyer will be here, too."

Chapter Four

The sidewalk teamed with lunch hour activity, crowded with people eager to take advantage of the perfect summer day. A good test for Pippin, Rylee brought both dogs along for the twenty-minute walk. Though his enthusiasm for the swirling throng tested Pippin's focus several times, he did well. Rylee wasn't surprised. Since coming to the academy two weeks ago, he proved both intelligent and eager to please. In fact, except for that disaster the other day with Elliott and Sil, which hadn't been the dog's fault, he responded to Rylee's intensified instruction like a willing student. It was time to bring in his owners.

She had some concerns with the Wilsons. While Bob Wilson remained indifferent to the family pet, Pippin intimidated Bob's wife Emily. Neither of them appeared capable, or willing, to project pack-leader status, which meant nothing but trouble considering Pippin's size. Unless the couple changed their behavior, no one would be happy. If that were the case, they would be better off finding Pippin another home—and getting themselves a cat. She planned to tell them just that and hoped the warning would sink in.

Rounding the corner onto Center Street, she spotted Brian's lanky six-foot frame. Affecting his typical, lazy slouch, he leaned against a rail fence enclosing a small courtyard. Behind him, a large brick

35

warehouse sat back from the street. Legs crossed at the ankles, he held a cell phone to his ear. A denim work-shirt rode his wide shoulders and chest, the sleeves rolled to the elbows, and a dusty smudge marred one thigh of his Khaki slacks. Scuffed work boots covered his large feet.

At her approach, he straightened and ended the call, slipping the phone into his pocket. A pair of aviator sunglasses hid his pale blue eyes and the sunlight brought out golden streaks in his mop of dark blond hair.

"I thought we were meeting the owner of the building." Rylee said in greeting. She directed the dogs to sit.

"He's late. And so are you."

"Couldn't be helped. Sil has her wand out again. I got away as quickly as I could."

White teeth flashed when he smiled. "You too? She tried to set me up with the meter maid who wrote her a ticket last week."

"What happened to…Karen? Last I heard you two were hot and heavy."

"She got pissed when she found out I'd been to a Yankee's game last week."

"Doesn't share your enthusiasm for the boys of summer, huh?"

"She doesn't share my enthusiasm for cheering on the boys while in the company of another woman."

"Wow. I didn't realize she was so shallow. What a bitch." Rylee offered the dry commiseration, crossing her arms. "You're better off without her."

He shrugged off the sarcasm. "Hey, Lucy tempted me with box seats. What can I say? I'm weak."

"What you are is a slut, and if Sil's trying to fix you up with meter maids it's your own fault. I refuse to feel sorry for you, especially since diffusing her matchmaking will take some of the pressure off of me."

They shared a grin.

She studied the two-story, brick structure. "So, this is it?"

He nodded. "The building is sixty-five years old, but the roof, electrical, and plumbing were all brought up to code less than five years ago. Plenty of parking out back. About the only exterior costs we'd see is if we decided to replace the windows."

"Do they need replacing?"

He tipped his flat hand back and forth.

"New windows, then."

She jumped when her cell phone vibrated in her pocket. Pulling it out, she frowned at the melodic chime of *Someday My Prince Will Come*. A quick glance at the caller ID showed a restricted call and she pressed the button, killing the song.

"Waiting on a prince?" Brian teased.

"I downloaded the tone last week to annoy Sil."

He snickered.

"Brian!"

He turned at the greeting and Rylee followed his gaze to find a hefty, middle-aged man in a rumpled suit hurrying down the sidewalk. His balding head gleamed with sweat and he huffed from exertion.

He shuffled to a stop before them. "Sorry I'm late."

"There's a lot of that going around." Brian winked at Rylee. "We just got here ourselves. Rip, this is Rylee Pierce, Silvia's niece. Rylee, Rip Cain."

"Hello, Mr. Cain." When he cast a wary glance at

the dogs, she reassured him. "They won't bother you."

"Rip, please." He smiled shyly. "I expected Silvia," he said to Brian. "I was looking forward to meeting her."

"She, ah, couldn't be here. Rylee will fill her in."

Rip nodded, his disappointment clear by his slumping shoulders. "Ah, well. To tell the truth, it's just as well. A bug is going around the travel agency and we're short-staffed. I need to get back." He reached inside his suit coat and pulled a key ring from his shirt pocket. "I just came by to give you the key. You can get it back to me later."

"That'll work."

Rip turned to Rylee. "I admire what your aunt and Brian are doing with their foundation. My sister's boy did three tours in Iraq before he came home for good. He and his family bought into the building over near the courthouse. They never could have afforded a place big enough for all of them without the foundation's help. You be sure to convey my thanks to Silvia."

"She'll be glad to hear it," Rylee said, smiling.

"You'll get back to me when you've made a decision?" he asked Brian.

"Silvia or I will be in touch."

"Good." He shook hands with Brian, nodded at Rylee and headed off down the sidewalk.

"Does it ever bother you?" Brian asked, watching him go. "That people don't know?"

"*I* know." And that was enough for her. "So, let's see if we've found our next building."

Waiting while he dealt with the lock and swung the door open, Rylee and the dogs went in first. They moved deep into the empty warehouse. A thin layer of dust coated the floor and windows. The stuffy odor of disuse hung in the air. Brian stood by the door, his hands on his hips.

"It's a clean slate." His voice echoed off the high ceiling. "Tear-out costs will be minimal. The square footage is right and the structure is solid."

"And the asking price?"

"A little steeper than I'd be willing to offer, but after being empty for years Rip is anxious to sell. He is serious about his admiration for the foundation. He's giving us a first shot before he puts it on the market."

He removed the sunglasses and his pale, blue gaze scanned the ten-foot ceiling.

"Bottom line?"

"Bottom line is we've looked at a lot of properties and this one has everything we're looking for. Unlike the occupants of our first two buildings, a couple of names on the list will need permanent access to the medical community. The VA is less than a mile away. Sil is working on a partnership with the medical center around the corner. The location is perfect. If Rip is willing to meet our price, this would be my choice."

Rylee glanced around the large warehouse space. Its purchase would take the foundation into new territory. Rehabbing the first two buildings hadn't been cheap, and the purchase and rehab of this one would come close to swallowing the rest of her initial investment. If Adam's House was to continue its mission, they were going to have to step up the fund-raising—starting with next month's event. But the investment would be worth the cost. Twenty deserving families could find a home here.

"Make the offer."

She shrieked when Brian crossed the distance on a steady stride, scooped her up in his arms and spun her around in a dizzying circle.

"Adam would be so proud of you," he said when he let her feet touch the ground.

She pushed out of his arms as both Pippin and her well-behaved Belle danced about them in excitement. "Quit it. You'll make me cry." She pointed at Pippin. "And that one freaks out when people cry."

"Rylee Pierce never cries." He grinned, tapping a finger to her nose while studying the moisture in her eyes. "She just mists."

"Damned straight," she agreed. Tagging along after Adam and Brian all those years taught Rylee to be tough and Ponzi Pete's little girl couldn't afford to show any kind of weakness.

"Have you eaten lunch?" he asked, leading her out the door and locking it behind them. She cast a pointed glance down at the dogs and he grinned. "There's a deli right around the corner. They have patio seating. We can test the pea brain's patience."

"Pippin doesn't have a pea brain," she cooed, rubbing the dog's ears. Brian cupped her elbow and started them in the direction of the deli, then hung back to let a group of teenagers pass by. When he stepped to her side again, she added, "And don't say things like that. You'll hurt his feelings."

"He doesn't understand a word I say. You're the only one around here who can talk to animals."

"We don't really talk to each other, I just understand them and they understand me."

They rounded the corner and approached the deli's outside seating. She dropped her outstretched arm then flicked up a palm. Without a word from her, both dogs dropped to the ground beside an open table.

Brian looked from the dogs to her, his smile wry. "Whatever you say, Ms. Doolittle. Pastrami, rye, right?"

Rylee licked her lips. "Mmm. Provolone, pickle, mustard."

"Be right back."

Five minutes later, they were sharing lunch beneath a blue and white striped umbrella. At her feet, Belle accepted the occasional notice of a passerby with her usual calm, while Pippin, whose sheer size tended to create a stir, required an occasional reminder to stay put. For an unplanned test, the results were promising, and reinforced Rylee's belief the time had come to bring in his family.

"So, Sil said she met Elliott's son this morning," Brian said around a mouthful of corned beef.

"Yep. He came by shortly after we got Elliott home from the hospital."

"You met him, too?"

She nodded, snagging a french fry from his plate.

"What's he like?"

She popped the fry into her mouth before answering. "Tall, dark, handsome. Typical run-of-the-mill movie star stuff."

Brian's blond brows rose. "I didn't ask what he *looked* like. I asked what he is *like*."

"Hmmm…" She took refuge in her mammoth sandwich and shrugged. "He's like a lawyer, I guess."

"You like him." He drew out the words in a teasing, singsong tone.

She pointed at his nose. "If you break into a verse

41

of *Rylee and Cooper Sitting in a Tree*, I'm going to slug you."

He burst out laughing and her scowl made him laugh harder. "There's nothing wrong with admitting you find a man attractive, Ry."

"Fine," she grumbled. "I thought he was hot, okay?"

Brian's eyes twinkled with continued amusement. "Is he single?" He bit off a hunk of his sandwich, speaking around the food. "You should ask him out."

She scowled. "You're as bad as Sil."

"Now, that's just mean, Rye Bread," he complained, using the nickname he and Adam annoyed her with when they were kids.

"Friendship has its privileges." She wiped her mouth with a napkin and leaned on her elbows. "I mean it, Bri. He's gorgeous and he's charming, just like Elliott. I have to admit, I'm tempted to break my own rule and go after him."

"So what's stopping you?"

"Really?" Her sarcasm dripped like ice cream melting from a cone.

"I'm serious. Elliott knows who you are and it doesn't bother him. Odds are his son won't care either."

"Elliott isn't a lawyer with the D.A.'s office. Besides, any guy who looks like Cooper Reed must have a girlfriend. For all I know he's married." The possibility made her frown.

"So find out," he suggested. "Sil could give you the scoop on him."

"And asking Sil about her stepson would get her off of your scent and onto mine."

"Two birds, one stone."

She rolled her eyes at his unapologetic grin. "Forget it."

"I could find out for you."

"Right. Then what? Are you going to pass me a note in study hall?"

He snickered and finished off the last bite of his sandwich. "Wouldn't be the first time."

"Nope." She shook her head. "He's Elliott's son, for heaven's sake. Can you imagine if I got involved with him and things got ugly when he found out about my dad? Sil would be pissed and Elliott caught in the middle. I'm not willing to chance that. I'll just have to admire him from afar."

"Coward."

"Pragmatist." Rylee smirked. "Now, are you going to buy me dessert?"

He eyed her empty plate. "I swear, Rye Bread, you can pack away food better than any woman I know, and a lot of the men."

"Cheesecake." She smiled sweetly when he rose from the table. "With strawberry topping!" she called as he disappeared inside.

Chapter Five

"Told you I could find out."

"Be quiet, you idiot."

Hands full, Rylee brushed by Brian to set the warm tray on the counter. She pealed the foil from Sil's Cajun kisses. The pungent vapor of shrimp-and-cheese-stuffed jalapeños teased her nostrils. She shot a glance toward the living area where Sil, Elliott, and Cooper Reed were engrossed in conversation.

"Thanks to your not-so-subtle probing," she complained under her breath, "Sil's wand is going to be working overtime." And if not for Sil's eagle-eyed interest, Rylee would have laughed her head off at Brian's conversational contortions, quizzing Coop on his relationship status. "Coop probably thinks you're gay, you know."

"Nah." A grin spread across Brian's face and he plucked a jalapeño from the full tray. "We men have radar about that kind of thing."

She snorted. "Some men may have gaydar, but from the way Coop was looking at you, he isn't one of them."

Brian avoided her slapping hand, snagging seconds.

"No wife, Rye Bread." He waggled the pilfered jalapeño in front of her nose. "The field is clear. Unless *he's* gay."

"Fat chance of that." Considering how his eyes cataloged every inch of her body that first day, she doubted there was anything gay about Cooper Reed. She smiled sweetly. "But that doesn't rule out a girlfriend."

His grin sharp, Brian lifted one shoulder in a lazy shrug. "Girlfriends can be replaced."

"Get away from me, Don Juan," she grumbled, hefting the tray. "And don't do me any more favors."

The sound of his wicked laughter followed her into the living room.

"Coop and I were just discussing next month's fundraiser." Sil looked over at Rylee's approach. "He has some connections in the city I'm hoping to tap."

She offered a bland smile in response. The foundation, or more precisely, her connection to it, was a subject she'd rather avoid while in the presence of an attorney with the D.A.'s office.

She set the tray on the coffee table. Brian dropped a pile of napkins beside it before seating himself in the last unoccupied chair. With Elliott and Sil cuddling on the couch, the only open seat was on the loveseat beside Coop. Rather than join him, Rylee rested a hip on the arm of Brian's chair, shoving back when he jabbed her in the ass with his elbow.

"I hadn't realized your aunt is *the* Silvia Burke, associated with The Adam's House Foundation," Coop told Rylee.

Rylee checked the chastising glare she wanted to send Sil's way. What could she be thinking, bringing up the foundation with Cooper Reed?

"You know of Adam's House?"

"Who doesn't?" He turned to Sil. "It was formed in

honor of your son from what I've read." Sil nodded. "I'm sure he'd be proud." He turned back to Rylee. "Affordable housing for returning combat vets is a worthy cause."

"Very worthy," she agreed.

"Coop has a contact in the fashion industry," Sil announced. "A couple of items from several designers would add definite New York panache to the silent auction, don't you think?"

Rylee bared her teeth in a warning smile, then turned to study Coop. "The fashion industry, huh? I wouldn't have thought a lot of high crimes and misdemeanors came out of the garment district."

"My connection with the fashion industry is more in the way of a personal association." He smiled, a slow curving of those perfectly cut lips below eyes twinkling with pure blue sin.

She'd just bet the association was personal. What woman could resist that deadly combination of I-want-to-taste-you lips and I-promise-you'll-enjoy-it eyes? Even though he was off limits, his bad boy smile made the breath back up in her throat. She swallowed against the heady rush swelling in her chest, competing for space with her constricting lungs.

To counter the corresponding breathlessness of her response, she cocked her head and crossed her arms. "With a model, no doubt."

"The contact I mentioned used to be a model."

She didn't spin around to smirk at Brian, but she wanted to. Instead, she settled for shoving an elbow at the shoulder closest to her hip.

"Now she's the personal assistant to one of the designers," Coop continued. "She and her husband are friends of mine."

Her ass received another jab, accompanied by Brian's self-satisfied grunt. She ignored both.

"I could introduce you to her if you'd like," Coop offered. "You could pitch her Silvia's fundraising idea."

Invitation filled the blue-sin gaze holding hers, for more than just a simple introduction to his friends.

She could almost hear Sil's silent urging. *Say yes, Rylee. Say yes!* Rylee refused to look her way. "Sil can pitch her own ideas. She handles the foundation's business. I train dogs."

She turned away at the unexpected flash of disappointment in Coop's eyes and the moment passed, but despite Rylee's lack of cooperation, Sil plowed ahead with her matchmaking strategy. Over the next hour, she grilled Coop on his life, interspersing her nosy questions with humorous memories from Rylee's childhood. Brian, the idiot, eagerly assisted.

Like a deviant tag-team, they traded stories of the juvenile pranks. Although Adam and Brian were the architects of most, Sil focused on Rylee's participation in their fiascos. Her aunt's agenda was so obvious, by the time dinner ended Rylee wanted to clobber Sil over the head with her fairy-godmother wand.

For his part, Coop appeared amused by Sil's blatant machinations. After that rejected invitation to meet his friends, he backed off from anything personal. He joined in the friendly banter around the table, laughing at himself as quickly as he did others, while Rylee wavered between relief and regret. But for the specter of her father's crimes, Coop was a man she would enjoy getting to know. Allowing herself that pleasure, however, would only end in disaster. One more disappointment to place at her father's feet.

Sil didn't share her concerns. When Rylee rose to slip downstairs to check on the dogs, Sil suggested Coop join her. To Rylee's surprise, he didn't hesitate, admitting a desire to meet the infamous Pippin.

"She's not very subtle, is she?" he said the moment the door shut behind them.

"No, she isn't." Rylee moved across the balcony and he followed. "Sorry about all of that." She tossed her head toward the condo door. "She can't help herself. Women born south of the Mason-Dixon Line carry a matchmaking gene." She paused at the top of the stairs. "Look, you don't have to do this. In fact, why don't you go back inside? It would serve Sil right to discover her plan has failed."

"Now, why would I do that?"

She blinked. Huh? What did he mean by that? He didn't want to hurt Sil's feelings by letting her know her plan hadn't worked? Or he didn't want to go back inside because he thought Sil's plan had merit? The first option made her heart pulse with approval, the second made it pound with panic. The competing erratic beats made her light-headed.

God, she needed a defibrillator.

But she wouldn't touch his comment with a ten-foot pole. She shrugged, starting down the stairs. "Suit yourself."

"She obviously loves you," he said, following. "And wants to see you happy."

"And I love her, but that doesn't mean I wouldn't enjoy strangling her sometimes."

His quiet chuckle wafted over her like a warm

breeze, and made the fine hairs on her arms stand at attention. She rolled her shoulders and hastened her descent to the first floor.

"She raised you, I gather?"

"From the time I was eleven."

"There's no family resemblance. Was her late husband your natural uncle?"

Rylee hesitated. She lived by the rule that the less people understood her familial ties, the better. Coop, however, was now a part of her extended family. The closer she stuck to the truth the better.

"Sil is my mother's cousin. She and Adam took me in and made me a part of their family when I was left alone." She reached the ground floor, pulled out her key and changed the subject. "Pippin is bound to be excited, so I apologize if he acts up a little. He's come a long way, but tends to forget his training when he's been left alone for any length of time."

She opened the door and stepped inside. Belle trotted out from the hallway, her docked tail ticking out her pleasure like a metronome on speed.

"There's my girl." Rylee rubbed the dog's side. The Boxer leaned against her leg in a body hug. Excited barking echoed from the back of the condo. "Pippin, quiet," Rylee called. The barking stopped.

"Nice trick." Coop shook the paw Belle offered, less reluctantly than the first time.

"Greeting someone properly is important to Belle. She's very polite."

"I meant the barking," he corrected, straightening.

She grinned. "I told you he'd be excited. Come on. I'll introduce you."

****

"Holy shit!"

Coop stopped just inside a room resembling a small pet store, without all the pets. Cages of various sizes lined the walls, from two-feet square to something he swore he'd seen on TV, lowered over the side of a boat by shark experts. The beast inside the shark cage all but danced in anticipation of his freedom.

"Sorry," he said belatedly. "But that is not a dog. That's a barnyard experiment gone wrong."

Rylee laughed, held out her arm and did something with her hand. The excited Great Dane dropped to his butt and waited while she worked the latch. In case the huge dog's docile behavior was a ruse, Coop scanned the room for possible weapons. None appeared, and even if one had, he wouldn't have had a chance to use it. The dog burst from the opened cage, knocking Rylee over in his haste, and charged Coop.

"Pippin!"

Rylee's shout barely registered as Coop stumbled backward and went down under the power of the dog's running leap. Belle's frantic barking added to the melee.

"Oh, God. Pippin!"

One hundred-sixty pounds of fur-covered muscle, lolling tongue, and sharp white teeth straddled Coop where he lay sprawled in the doorway. To his relief, the dog didn't use the teeth. The tongue was another story.

"Pippin, back," Rylee commanded.

Doing his best to dodge Pippin's sloppy lashing, Coop caught a glimpse of Rylee, crawling across the floor on her hands and knees. Pippin landed one last, wet swipe to Coop's chin before he managed to get hold of the dog's collar. Straightening his arms and sitting up, Coop forced the dog back several steps. Rylee reached for Pippin's collar, scrambling to her feet and tugging him back even farther.

"Oh, dear God, are you all right?" Her eyes were wide with dismay. "Did he hurt you?"

"Only my pride." Coop used his sleeve to wipe his face.

"I am so sorry."

"I'm fine, Rylee," he tried to reassure her, but she spoke over him.

"He's still struggling with jumping when he's excited, but he's never done anything like that before. Are you sure you aren't hurt?"

Coop climbed to his feet, dusting himself off. "I'm fine."

Pippin yanked and twisted, trying to break her grip. "Pippin, heel!"

"Let him go."

"No way in hell." Eyes saucer-big, she turned her body to block the excited dog. "He wasn't trying to hurt you, Coop. I'll just put him back in the cage until you're gone."

"I realize that, Rylee, but *he* needs to know he can't do that type of thing."

"I agree, but—"

"He didn't tackle *you*, Rylee. Let him go."

Indecision shadowed her eyes and she shook her head.

"He'll be fine. I promise. Just let him go. Now."

She swallowed, her gaze darting down to the straining dog and back. "Easy Pippin," she soothed. Despite her obvious unease, she uncurled her fingers from the thick collar.

The Great Dane bounded across the space in a flash. Excitement shone in his ebony eyes. His muscles bunched as he leapt. Coop stepped aside and flung out his arm, clotheslining the beast. The jolt ricocheted up Coop's shoulder. Stopped short, Pippin slammed to the floor. Coop followed, straddling him before the dog could scramble back to his feet.

"Down," Coop said sharply. After several long moments, the dog stopped struggling and dropped his large head to the floor. His chest heaved from exertion, but he relaxed. "Stay."

Coop rose to his feet. Pippin didn't move.

Rylee stared open-mouthed. "If things don't work out for you in the D.A.'s office," she said, "you've got yourself a job here anytime." He chuckled and her smile came slow. "Where did you learn to do that?"

"I did several ride-alongs with NYPD when I first joined the D.A.'s office. Two of those days were with a K-9 unit. I picked up a few things."

She eyed Pippin, who still hadn't moved. "For someone who doesn't like dogs, you have the touch."

"Who said I don't like dogs?"

"The other day, when I explained that your father was hurt because he saved Pippin." She paused at his lifted brow. "Never mind. First impressions." She shrugged. "So, are you going to let him up?"

"Go ahead," he invited.

She shook her head. "You gave the order to stay. You finish it. And make sure to praise him. He's sensitive."

"Sensitive hell, he's psychotic," Coop grumbled then patted his thigh. "Pippin, come here, boy."

Pippin jumped up and moved to Coop's side. His

head hung low as he approached and Coop figured she had it right. The dog was either embarrassed or cowered.

"Good boy." Coop scrubbed the dog's large head and Pippin's tongue snuck out for a lick.

Rylee gripped the dog's collar and grimaced. "We're still working on the kissing."

Coop hesitated at the irresistible opening. "Let me know if I can be of any help with that."

Chapter Six

Rylee reacted to Coop's suggestive comment exactly as he expected. She blinked and a tiny frown creased her brow. Whenever the conversation veered toward anything even remotely personal, either she fell back on that sarcastic wit she'd perfected or she retreated into silence. Like now.

Curious contradictions lurked beneath the carefree, lighthearted image she projected. She'd dismissed his show of interest, along with his invitation to meet his friends, and yet he caught her watching him several times during dinner, her eyes full of feminine awareness. Her aunt's matchmaking annoyed her, but she smiled and teased him, including him in the family camaraderie around the table.

Confusion trumped wariness in her eyes now. He'd thrown her off-balance. Good. Since meeting her the other day, she'd been popping into his head with annoying regularity. Why should he be alone in his madness?

He'd been anxious to see her again, telling himself he'd imagined the unprecedented sexual pull he'd experienced for Elliott's stepdaughter, step-cousin—step-whatever. His imagination was in play, all right. From the moment he'd seen her again, he'd envisioned her in a number of different situations. She'd been naked in all of them.

And he wasn't the only one experiencing the pull. Those flashes of feminine awareness in her dark-chocolate eyes broadcast her attraction to him, an attraction she evidently planned to ignore. He'd see about that. He hadn't earned his reputation as a successful prosecutor by backing away from a difficult case, and the beautiful dog trainer was a case he meant to crack.

He turned away and wandered further into the room. Pippin trotted at his side.

"So, this is The Canine Academy?" He eyed the cages. "Where are your other students?"

A soft release of pent up breath reached his ears and he smiled. Yes, off balance was just how he wanted her.

"Gone for the day."

"Why is Pippin still here?"

"Pippin required a more intense program. He's our only boarder at the moment."

"Have dinner with me," he said, without turning around. She didn't answer and he waited several beats before glancing over his shoulder. Her eyes shuttered, she fell back on sarcasm.

"We just finished dinner. What do you have, a tapeworm?"

He faced her. "I'd like to take you to dinner, Rylee."

Her hand went to Belle's head beside her and she jutted her chin up a notch. "That wouldn't be a good idea, Coop."

"Why? I'm attracted to you, and a man can tell when the attraction is mutual."

She said nothing, returning his gaze while she

scratched the fur between Belle's ears.

"It's just a meal." He crossed his arms. "I'm not suggesting we jet off to Vegas."

She snorted softly. "That's a relief. Casinos give me a headache."

The dry sarcasm made him smile. She hadn't said no.

"Look, you're a great-looking guy."

He flashed a grin, pleased when her lips twitched in response.

"And I admit you have a certain amount of charm."

"But?"

"But, your father is married to my aunt."

"Your mother's cousin," he corrected. He dropped his arms to his sides and stepped toward her. "And Dad and Silvia can get their *own* dinner."

Her lips formed a genuine smile, but she shook her head. "People rarely come out of this kind of thing on friendly terms."

"This kind of thing?" He continued to advance.

"We're connected through Sil and Elliott. I don't want to see them caught in the middle when this...dating thing, or whatever it is you're after, ends."

"This dating thing?"

"Or whatever it is you're after," she repeated. As he closed the distance, she stepped back and bumped up against the shark cage. She slapped her spread fingers against his chest to prevent him from coming any closer. "I'm not in the market for a relationship right now."

"Then we don't have a problem, because neither am I." He brushed a fingertip over the perfect skin of her cheekbone. "So, here's what I suggest."

Her eyelids fluttered, pupils dilating, and reluctant temptation replaced the wariness in her dark orbs. Still, she kept a defensive hand on his chest.

"If you insist on negotiating when I've already explained my concerns," she said, holding his gaze, "I'd rather you didn't touch me."

He checked the urge to kiss her at the artless admission of finding his touch disturbing. Instead, he moved his hand to the cage beside her head. He wrapped his fingers around the metal bar and dipped his head, bringing his face closer to hers. She blinked but held her ground, boldly meeting his gaze.

"I propose we get to know one another," he pressed. "A few dinners. Maybe a show, or a ball game or two if you like. We find out what makes each other tick."

"Hmmm." Her mouth moved into a smirk. "Five seconds ago you were talking a meal. Now it's a few dinners and a ball game or two. At this rate we'll be jetting off to Vegas by the end of the week."

She didn't try to stop him when he took the final step that brought their bodies within inches of each other. "Has anyone ever accused you of being a wiseass?"

Head cocked as though considering the question, her mouth quivered on a smile. "Nope."

"How about a liar?"

She lost the battle with the smile and her low laugh sent a lash of desire whipping across his midsection. He did what he'd wanted to do since arriving at his father's condo days ago. Leaning in, he took...

****

Mistake. Mistake. Mistake.

The chant echoed in her head.

Except this didn't feel like a mistake. No, this was amazing, and exciting, and…oh, God, so good!

She'd been kissed before. Hell, she'd been engaged, but none of those mouth-to-mouth exercises she shared with Marcus ever came close to this. Compared to Cooper Reed, Marcus kissed like a dead fish.

Skipping right past nice-to-meet-you, Coop jumped straight into an I-couldn't-wait-another-moment-to-taste-you devouring. He didn't fumble or grab like some of the men she'd dated. His mouth moved over hers with confident intent in a slow, thorough exploration. The fine hairs on her body lifting as if brushed by an electrical charge. Goose bumps rose and left her chilled, despite the heat of his mouth threatening to burn her alive. He touched her nowhere else, but that didn't matter. She sensed the caress of his mouth all over, as though she were already naked and spread out for his pleasure.

His lips nibbled and tasted, and when his tongue teased the seam of her lips in a silken caress, she opened her mouth, granting him entrance. His low growl of approval spurred her on and she met his bold foray. Tongues tangling, she thrilled to the strength of his muscled arms wrapping around her and pulling her close.

Mistake!

Some rogue neurotransmitter managed to pierce the hazy bubble of lust threatening to carry her away. The warning shrieked through her brain and she fought against the accompanying panic. Frustration joined the party. There had to be a workable solution, because nothing so pleasant could be wrong.

But the damage was done. She pulled back, her eyelids fluttering open to find his passion-darkened eyes gleaming inches above hers.

"We need to add an addendum to our negotiation." The low rumble of his voice vibrated through her breasts, crushed to his chest.

She swallowed before she could speak. "Addendum?"

"I think we should add some time in bed to that list of get-to-know-you activities."

Despite the erratic beat of her heart, she couldn't help but smile, which increased her panic. A man who could ignite her body with a kiss *and* tickle her funny bone would be hazardous to her equilibrium, and his position with the D.A.'s office made Cooper Reed downright dangerous to the life she'd fought so hard to build. Considering how easily he managed to make her forget that fact, she'd be wise to keep her distance— which wouldn't be easy, not with the memory of that kiss jabbing at her.

He had just proven his ability to smash through the barriers she threw up. If she didn't do the smart thing, staying as far away from him as possible, she'd be fighting both Coop and herself, when what she really wanted was to take a chance and see where this explosive attraction between them led.

"Coop." She dropped her forehead to his chest for just a moment before pressing him back a step. She rested against the bars, grateful for the cage's support considering the unsteadiness of her legs.

"Rylee," he echoed, letting her go.

"Like I said, this isn't a good idea."

His steady gaze held hers. "You said dinner wasn't a good idea. But this," he waved a hand back and forth between them, "this is something else. A woman doesn't kiss a man the way you just kissed me if she thinks ending up in bed with him is a bad idea."

"She does if she's stupid," she grumbled then rolled her eyes. "And you're being purposefully obtuse. You know what I mean."

"What I am being is argumentative. I don't understand what the problem is, unless you already have a man in your life. Are you and Brian…?"

The absurdity of the suggestion was too much. "Oh," she snickered. "Brian would bust a gut laughing if he knew you were thinking that. And no, Brian and I are not involved. He's practically my brother."

"Then like *I* said, we don't have a problem."

She disagreed, but wasn't about to squabble with a professional arguer. Anything she might say to make her case would be a waste of breath. She crossed her arms.

"I get what you're saying about Sil and my father, Rylee. I don't want them hurt, either. We've established that neither of us is interested in a relationship, not in the typical sense anyway. We're two unattached adults suffering from a case of mutual attraction, and I can't see any reason why we shouldn't act on that attraction and enjoy each other's company for a time. With," he added, raising a hand when she started to object, "an agreement from the beginning that when it's over, we walk away friends. No hard feelings allowed."

To enjoy him without worrying about potential, ugly fallout? What a heady temptation. Excitement coursed through her at the scenario he described, her willpower no match for the lure of the untold pleasures shining in his eyes.

No wonder he thrived in his chosen career. The ability to calmly argue his point, combined with those sexy, dark good looks, would sway any jury to his side.

"You sound like a lawyer," she complained, because she was going to agree to his irresistible proposal, despite knowing she would most likely pay a price in the end.

"And you are beautiful."

Warmth flooded her body at his softly spoken compliment. The man would charm her out of her panties before she had the chance to blink. Well, she'd be losing them eventually, but they'd be establishing some boundaries before her underwear went anywhere.

"For a time?" she asked.

"Until one or both of us decides the time has come to walk away."

"And until that happens, we're exclusive." She frowned. "When I decide to sleep with a man, I don't like to share." Since she had slept with no man but Marcus, and being a cheater wasn't one of his faults, she'd never given the need to demand exclusivity a thought. It bothered her that she did now.

White teeth flashed when he grinned. His gaze roamed her body before he answered. "Believe me, Rylee, another woman is not going to be a problem."

Maybe not for him, but the man was a walking, talking, sexual fantasy. For reasons he didn't understand, and with any luck never would, their association would be short-lived. She did not intend to spend a good portion of their limited time together dealing with potential competitors for his attention.

Thrilled at the promise in his eyes, she lifted a brow and waited.

"Exclusivity goes both ways."

"That goes without saying." She waved a hand. "We part as friends, doing everything possible to make sure Sil and Elliott don't get caught in any kind of crossfire."

He nodded.

"Well, then." She heaved a breath. "I guess the negotiations are complete." Now that they were, her heart raced like a runaway train, and she had no idea what they were supposed to do next. "I've never negotiated this type of thing before. What do we do now?"

He chuckled and brushed a fingertip over the curve of her cheek. "First, we relax. This doesn't have to be complicated, Rylee. Don't over think it."

"That's easy for you to say. I'm about to have a heart attack."

He laughed and bending, brushed his lips over hers once more. He straightened before the heat between them could explode out of control.

"We'll start with that meal. How does your schedule look tomorrow? Can you meet me for lunch? Say, around one?"

"I could do that."

"Good. What's your cell number?" He unclipped the phone from his belt.

She recited the number and he punched at the keypad, placing a call. Her annoy-Sil ringtone chimed. She scrambled to pull the phone from her pocket.

"Disney fan or are you a romantic?" he asked, grinning.

She jammed her thumb down on the power button. Disney could have used Coop's likeness for one of their animated princes. With his head of thick, dark hair and the toothy grin on his handsome face, he had the look.

"Neither," she said. "Long story."

"Okay, Snow White," he chuckled at her smirk, "you have my number. Call me tomorrow and I'll let you know what time I'll be free from court." He clipped his phone back on his belt. "Thank Silvia for me, will you? Her jambalaya is the best I've ever tasted."

"You're leaving?" The question came out as a squeak.

"I'm giving you a little space to get used to the idea of you and me."

"Oh."

Confusion beetled her brows. Agreeing with his suggestion that they get to know one another was a big frigging deal, at least for her, and he wanted to leave? Maybe she had misread his signals after all, despite that heated kiss.

He took the small step needed to bring their bodies flush once again. Sandwiched between the bars of the cage and his muscled body, she couldn't miss one very prominent signal pressed against her belly. She stared up into his heated gaze.

"Unless you're willing to join me in that bed we discussed right now, I'm going home to take a cold shower."

Tempted to suggest he use her shower *after* she joined him in the bed just down the hall, she nodded instead. "That might be best."

"Then I'll look forward to your call tomorrow." He stepped back, his intent blue gaze roaming her face before he turned on his heel and left.

She called Pippin back when he tried to follow.

Chapter Seven

The restaurant, upscale and crowded despite the traditional noon rush having passed more than two hours earlier, charmed Rylee with its welcoming atmosphere. She swiveled her head, absorbing every aspect of the converted carriage house as she followed the maitre d' to a secluded table near the back. Coop rose at their approach, a slow smile spreading across his face, and nerves tap-danced over Rylee's spine. She smiled and thanked the maitre d' when he held out her chair.

"Sorry, I'm late," she said once they were alone. "My appointments ran a little long this morning."

And the last one had been worth the delay. As long as the multiple inspections of the Cain warehouse came back clean, Adam's House would have its next building, at a price they could afford.

"I just got here myself," Coop replied. "Thanks for meeting me."

"You promised me a meal." She curved her lips in a subtle challenge. "Several, if I recall.

"And I always keep my promises." He grinned and held out the bottle of wine for her inspection. She nodded and he filled her glass.

The light in his eyes spoke of promises other than food and she suppressed a shiver of anticipation. Having an affair with an assistant district attorney may not be the wisest thing she would ever do, but considering the zing of pleasure careening through her system simply from sitting at a table with him, the risk would be worth the potential fallout.

"This is my first time here." She picked up her wine, glancing around. Fresh flowers adorned the linen-covered tables. Candlelight created a cozy ambiance, as did the soothing notes of the baby grand piano in the center of the room, tinkling beneath the quiet murmur of conversation. She met his gaze. "It's lovely."

"Like you."

The compliment made her grin. "Nice line, councilor."

Humor sparkled in his eyes over the rim of his wineglass. "No line." He set the glass aside and picked up his menu. "Simple truth. Shall we order?"

He asked after her day while they waited for the arrival of their lunches, and she reciprocated, intrigued to learn he'd spent the morning dealing with the suspected Queen's arsonist. A string of fires had troubled the burrow over the summer. The pre-dawn blazes were the result of Molotov cocktails tossed from a passing car into vacant buildings. Dismissed at first as random pranks by kids, the charge elevated to murder when one of the targeted buildings wasn't empty after all. Two homeless men perished in the fire.

"I'm glad they finally got him," she said, suppressing a shudder. "So many fires in such a short time have left people jumpy."

Coop nodded, waiting until the waiter delivered their plates and left. "What made you decide on dog training?"

"It was more a natural progression than a

decision." The savory aroma of pasta with red peppers and basil teased her nose, making her mouth water. She forked up a bite. "Heavenly," she moaned and licked her lips. "When I was twelve years-old, I found a stray dog living in the woods behind our house. One of his legs was broken. A car hit him, I think. I knew nothing about dogs, but I couldn't leave him to suffer."

"You kept him?"

She nodded. "For three days I worked to gain his trust. Once I had, I snuck him into the house and cleaned him up. When Sil found out she pitched a fit, but I just couldn't let the poor thing struggle on his own. He'd already been through enough. Long story short, Adam and I convinced Sil we needed a dog and Tri became a member of the family."

"Tri?"

"The leg needed to be amputated, but that didn't slow him down. He was the fastest thing on three legs, and the first of many strays I collected. I managed to find homes for most of them, and word of my ability with dogs got around. I earned my first dollar training Mrs. Olsen's poodle to stop digging up her rose beds."

He propped his elbows on the table. "So, a psychotic Great Dane is a natural progression from three legged mutts and digging poodles?"

"Pippin isn't psychotic," she argued, but smiled.

"All evidence to the contrary."

"He responded readily enough when you took control of the situation." She mirrored his elbows on the table and leaned forward. "I was very impressed."

He dropped his head slightly, shrinking the distance between them. "I was trying to impress the idiot dog. You're admiration is a bonus."

Their gazes tangled across the table and she welcomed the delicious spark of sexual tension flaring between them.

"Well," she cleared her throat, "you managed both."

"Is that why you agreed to our...dating thing? Because of my impressive handling of a wild animal?"

She grinned into his laughing blue gaze. "Of course. But what really impressed me was that you didn't scream like a girl when Pippin knocked you on your ass."

He chuckled and she sat back, picking up her wine glass. "The point is with the right handling, Pippin will make a great family pet."

"For a family of lion tamers, maybe."

"I shouldn't laugh since I've had the same thought. Oh, not that he needs a lion tamer, but he *will* need someone assertive enough to handle his size and zest for life. I'm not sure assertive applies to his owner. Mrs. Wilson is intimidated by him."

"Why would she choose such a monster if she's afraid of him?"

"I have no idea, although he wasn't a monster when she got him."

"What will happen to him if she decides he's too much for her?"

"I won't let anything happen to him. Though I try to avoid emotional attachments with my charges, I have to admit, Pippin has wormed his way into my heart. If things don't work out with the Wilsons, I'll find him another home." She cocked her head, studying him. "He likes *you*. In fact—"

"Oh, no." Coop shook his head, shutting her down.

"The only member of The Canine Academy I'm interested in is its owner."

"Hmmm…" She made her sigh a subtle tease. "Well, that's too bad. Handling a wild animal may impress me, but I'm a complete sucker for a guy with a dog."

His low laugh brought about the return of that electrical charge she'd experienced yesterday, and her nipples pebbled beneath the confines of her blouse and bra. She marveled at his ability to touch her without lifting a finger, but his next words almost made her spew wine across the table.

"How did you come to be raised by Sil?"

Well, crap. That didn't take long.

What had she been thinking? They would proceed with this dating thing without any of the usual get-to-know-you questions? Cutting her losses and walking away before the whole situation blew up in her face would be the best course. But damn it, she didn't want to walk away. Not yet. Evasion was her best option.

"Sil and Adam were the only family I had left," she said, and then quickly asked, "What about you? Sil says Elliott and you moved around a lot while you were growing up. What was that like?"

****

"I wasn't implying we should stop seeing each other, Cooper. I was upset. You know it was a big night for me. Even Giovanni wondered where you were."

"Did you tell him I was in Chicago, making sure a murderer doesn't walk free?"

At her irritated sigh, Coop wondered, and not for the first time, why either of them allowed their association to continue so long. Other than the sex, in the two years he and Ashley Connor dated, they hadn't seen eye-to-eye on much, including the amount of time he spent doing his job. Frankly, there were times he wasn't sure she even liked him.

After having spent time with Rylee, with her easy smiles, sarcastic wit, dark-secret eyes and gut-wrenching walk, he had to admit, he didn't particularly like Ashley either. The cynical convenience that defined his and Ashley's relationship left a bitter film in his throat. His connection to one of the most sought-after women on several continents had been a stroke to Coop's ego. For Ashley, Coop's political connections were the main source of appeal. But using wasn't the same as caring.

Exclusivity played no role in their relationship. Unlike Rylee, the word wasn't in Ashley's vocabulary. On the road more often than not, Giovanni's favorite model seduced men worldwide, and too many beautiful women wandered the streets of Manhattan for Coop to be content twiddling his thumbs while awaiting Ashley's return.

"Why don't you ask Giovanni to take you tomorrow night?" he suggested. "He'll know everyone and I'm sure he'll enjoy himself more than I would."

"He's already going," she snapped. "Besides, he's gay, darling," she added more evenly.

"And your point is? It's an industry event, not a candlelit dinner for two."

"Why are you being difficult? I said I was sorry."

"I'm being reasonable. I don't see the point of dragging this out when we both knew all along what we had together was never going to go anywhere."

"You're right," she sniffed. "I'd prefer attending

alone to spending another interminable evening with a workaholic bore who can't tell the difference between discount catalog and couture."

He chuckled at her peevish tone. "Point taken. Take care of yourself, Ashley."

"You're dumping me?" Incredulity rang in her clipped demand.

"I thought we came to that mutual decision the last time we spoke, but if it makes you feel better, consider me the dumpee in this case."

"Oh, I do, you bastard." Her hard-won cultured accent disappeared beneath a nasal Bronx snarl. "Nobody dumps Ashley Connor."

The call clicked off, and knowing Ashley, she'd be picking up a new phone to replace the one she just shattered against the wall of her Park Avenue townhouse. Pissed, her ego tweaked, she would fume for a while, but a new man would be warming her bed before the end of the week. He put her out of his mind, an easy task since the moment he'd knocked on Elliott's door and gotten an eyeful of Rylee Pierce.

He'd endured several teasing comments from Tim this week, remarking on his preoccupation with the sultry dog trainer. His friend lifted a knowing brow when Coop requested Tim include Rylee in his investigation after all.

"The bigger they are, the harder they fall," he insisted, laughing.

Coop didn't bother correcting Tim's assumption. The truth was, she intrigued him, and not just because he desperately wanted her in his bed.

Rylee Pierce had secrets.

At lunch earlier in the week, she displayed a warm

and funny personality, and showed genuine interest when the topic turned to his career. A smartass dog trainer one moment, a sexy seductress the next, he was charmed...until the moment he inquired as to how she'd come to be raised by Silvia. Her eyes went flat and she looked as though she wanted to bolt. She changed the subject, her evasion clumsy, and he let it go. For the time being.

As a prosecutor, he understood appearances could be deceiving. Most people had something in their background they would rather not have exposed to the public, but he couldn't imagine what that something might be in Rylee's case. A straightforward woman with a giving nature, she hadn't set off any of the internal alarms he'd come to trust after dealing with scumbags for so long. Still, she was hiding something. By nature and profession, he needed to discover what that something was.

Negotiating in her kennel, she insisted their *dating thing* end when one of them decided to walk away. When, at the end of their lunch, she once again expressed her doubts about their association, he suspected she planned to make use of their walk-away-as-friends clause sooner rather than later. She balked, but eventually agreed to a second date, for dinner the next night.

As skittish as she was, his best plan of attack would be to slow things down and avoid those topics that set her off. He hadn't mistaken the sensual expectancy in her eyes, despite the occasional flash of panic. Desire to keep her secrets battled with old-fashioned lust, and while he suspected the private side of her considered cutting and running, the sensual side responded helplessly to every carnal lure he tossed out, leaving him all but sweating in anticipation.

Gaining her trust was the key to overcoming her wariness, and if that meant pulling back and letting her call the shots for the time being, he'd do it. In the meantime, he was beginning to detest cold showers.

****

Emily Wilson jumped and her startled yelp echoed across the yard when Pippin bumped her thigh.

Rylee gritted her teeth. "Pack leader, Emily. Remember?"

The academy's morning class had ended ten minutes earlier. Sil returned upstairs to check on Elliott, while Rylee remained for some one-on-one time with Pippin and Emily. So far, the exercise produced nothing but anxiety for both dog and owner. The tiny brunette clutched the leash so tightly her knuckles were white. Pippin all but danced at her side.

"He's gotten so big," Emily complained, tugging at his leash. "I just can't handle him."

"He's a Great Dane. Of course he's big."

Rylee moved toward them while giving Pippin the signal to stay. His visible quivering broadcast an imminent mutiny. A horrifying vision of Pippin dragging Emily Wilson across the exercise yard like a rag doll tethered to the tail of a manic kite flashed in Rylee's head. She hurried her steps, not surprised when Emily thrust the leash into her hand and scrambled back.

"Dogs don't stay puppies forever, Emily. What were you expecting?"

"I guess I didn't think it through," she admitted, her face pale in the morning sunlight.

Rylee didn't bother agreeing with the woman's understatement. "Why would you choose such a large breed if his size is a problem?"

"When I was growing up the woman in the next apartment owned a Great Dane. They always looked so regal together. A Great Dane makes a statement."

"A dog isn't a statement. A dog is a commitment and a member of the family."

"I realize that. Now." Emily's guilty grimace set off warning bells in Rylee's head. "Unfortunately, that member-of-the-family part is a problem," she added.

"How so?"

She rested a hand on her belly. "Bob and I just discovered we're pregnant. We don't think we'll be comfortable having Pippin in the house once the baby comes."

Though not unexpected, the announcement angered Rylee. Too often people took on the responsibility of an animal then cast that responsibility aside when things proved complicated. Normally she took this type of thing in stride, but this was Pippin. She glanced down at him and anger bumped into dismay at the plea in his soulful, brown eyes.

She doesn't want me.

Rylee scratched at a spot behind his left ear, the way he liked. "What are you going to do with him?"

Emily's eyes held embarrassed anticipation. "We were hoping you'd have a suggestion."

As though following the conversation, the Great Dane leaned against Rylee's thigh and she sighed. "I'll need his papers."

Emily's shoulders slumped with relief. "They're in my purse."

"You brought them with you?" Rylee shook her head. *What? Did she have* "Sucker for troubled Great Danes" *written on her forehead?* "What would you have done if I'd said I couldn't help?"

"To tell you the truth, I'm not sure. I've been in touch with a woman at a local Great Dane rescue, but I wanted to speak to you first. You've done wonders with him and I can see you love him. Despite what you think, I love him, too."

When Pippin pressed even closer, Rylee looked down to find him watching her.

She doesn't love me enough.

"Are you sure about this, Emily? The birth of the baby is a long way off and he's smart. With a little bit of effort on your part—"

"I'm sure," she interrupted. "Bob and I agree this is for the best."

"Well, then. We may as well go get those papers." Emily fell into step at Rylee's side. Angry despite the resignation, yet admittedly a bit relieved, she cast a disgruntled glance Emily's way. "I'm not refunding his tuition."

"I wasn't going to ask." Emily met her gaze and smiled. "Thank you, Rylee. I know you're angry and you have every right to be." She rubbed Pippin's sleek back. "He really is a sweetheart. I'm kind of hoping you'll decide to keep him yourself, but if not, I know you'll find him a good home."

Twenty minutes later, Rylee tossed her cell phone on her desk and flopped back in the chair. "Don't look at me like that."

Across the room, Pippin stared at her, accusation shining in his eyes.

"It's not like I'm tossing you out. I'm just making inquiries. You need a family. One with a little boy, maybe, who'll need you to take care of him and love him as much as he'll love you. If I kept every dog I came across who needed a home, I'd end up on the news like one of those crazy animal hoarders."

But, I'm special.

She sighed. Yes, Pippin was special. Her connection with certain dogs was more intense than with others, a distinction she contributed to the animal's intelligence. The whispering, as people referred to her unusual ability with dogs, normally manifested as a vague impression of the animal's emotions. The link she and Pippin shared held no such ambiguity. His thoughts were as clear as if he spoke them aloud. Brian's Doctor Doolittle comment wasn't far off the mark in Pippin's case.

As a nod to her responsibility as a professional dog trainer, she'd made the calls, inquiring after suitable placement, but she'd simply been going through the motions. Just as she'd anticipated the Wilsons' ultimate decision to let Pippin go, she'd known she couldn't do the same. Sil would roll her eyes, but she wouldn't be surprised to learn Pippin would be joining the family.

Rylee pointed at him. "I'm pack-leader, buster. What I say goes." Joyful hope gleamed in his eyes. Rylee glanced toward the doorway and a vision of Pippin pinning Coop to the floor flashed through her head. "If you're going to be sticking around, there are rules. And number one is no more jumping!"

He immediately came to his feet, padding around her desk to rest his muzzle against the crook of her arm. He brushed his large head against her in his version of a hug.

I love you.

A fatalistic smile curved her mouth and she leaned down to rest her forehead against his.

"I love you, too."

Chapter Eight

"Wow!"

Coop's low compliment, echoed in his appreciative eyes, brushed over Rylee's nerve endings like a caress.

"The exact reaction I was shooting for," she said, smiling up at him where he stood framed in the open doorway.

"Mission accomplished."

After the stress she suffered over her choice of dress for tonight's date, his reaction thrilled her down to her toes. Classy casual, he'd said of the dress code for the retirement party they were to attend, and she'd settled on a little black dress that left her shoulders bare and skimmed her legs to mid-thigh. She'd gone for simplicity rather than sexy, but from his response, she'd achieved both.

She let her gaze roam over his stark black attire. "You're not so bad yourself."

Talk about understatements. Leashed power came to mind. The collarless, black silk shirt, tucked into fitted black slacks, framed the tapered broadness of his chest, trim hips and long legs with mouth-watering results. She recalled describing him to Brian as movie star handsome. Tonight, he could've stolen the show on any of those red carpets Hollywood loved to roll out.

She stepped back, silently inviting him inside. Coop followed, craning his neck to check the hallway.

"He's not here." Rylee grinned. "Neither is Belle. Brian has them. He has a date with a dog lover and borrowed them as props."

"The man's a masochist," he muttered.

She chuckled. "He practically grew up in Sil's house so he knows how to handle dogs, but he may agree with that sentiment by the end of the night. Pippin was a wriggling mass of excitement when they left."

"Do you loan out your client's animals often?"

She crossed to the foyer table to scoop up her clutch purse and a light shawl. "That's the thing. As of this morning, Pippin is no longer my client's animal. He's mine." When she turned back, his eyes twinkled with humor.

"Still collecting strays?"

She joined him at the door. "I can't seem to help myself. And you're lucky Pippin isn't here. He'd have a problem with that label."

He grinned and bent to press his mouth to hers. Relief made her lightheaded. Her toes curled in her shoes at the rush of excitement racing through her system. Since that mind-blowing kiss in the kennel, he'd been keeping his distance, physically speaking. A state of affairs she found both confusing and frustrating.

He'd knocked her off-balance with his bold come-on. Despite her better judgment, she'd committed to exploring the irresistible magnetism between them. Her natural wariness hadn't stood a chance against the smoldering promise in his eyes, but the passionless pecks he'd been doling out ever since failed to deliver on that promise. She'd gone back to wondering if she'd read him wrong after all.

But this, oh this...finally!

She combusted under his kiss. Heat and yearning converged, spreading outward from their fused lips to touch off hot spots as a brushfire of hunger consumed her. Sizzling fingers of pleasure drew a moan from her throat and she pressed close to his hard frame.

He answered her unspoken invitation without hesitation, his arms coming around her until he surrounded her with his strength and warmth. His tongue invaded her mouth like a marauder. Fingers spread, his palm rode the curve of her spine, sliding downward. The top of her head nearly popped off when those long fingers skimmed her tailbone to mold over one cheek of her butt. He squeezed the curve and her hips arched, bringing her into delicious contact with the hard evidence of his reaction to their thrilling embrace.

Finally, her mind repeated. *Oh, finally.*

A moment later, she discovered her relief was premature. He abruptly broke the kiss, lifting his head, and dropped his arms from around her to step back. Denied his support, she locked her knees in an effort to avoid sliding to the floor on legs turned to gelatin.

Breathing heavy, they stared at each other, her eyes wide, his narrowed and hooded. A moment passed before she caught her breath.

"Not that I'm complaining," she breathed, "but what was that for?"

"No reason, other than you're lovely. I'll be the envy of every man there tonight."

The slight roughness of his voice did nothing to dowse the fire he'd sparked within her, but knowing she wasn't alone in her discomfort was gratifying. Before she gave into temptation, suggested they skip tonight's party and get back to stoking that fire, she heaved a cleansing breath.

"Why, Mister Reed," she teased, letting her southern roots draw out the syllables. "You say the sweetest things."

Chest expanding with his own cleansing breath, he curled his lips in a wry smile. "Are you ready to go?"

She nodded, and by the time they arrived at the Irish pub just outside Time's Square, the fire within her had cooled to embers, but fanning them back to life wouldn't take much. Coop, on the other hand, appeared to have put the incident behind him. Cool and in control once again, he escorted her around the pub where she met many of his co-workers and friends.

"Coop says you're a dog whisperer." Lilly Watson grinned at Coop's startled glance. "What? You did!" Beside her, Tim Watson attempted to hide a grin, his prizefighter's face softening with humor as he winked at his slim, blonde wife.

Coop had introduced the couple as friends. Lilly, he explained, was the ex-model he'd spoken of in Elliott's living room the night he'd come to dinner, and Tim worked with him at the D.A.'s office. Based on the flow of conversation over the last hour, their friendship was close. They traded amusing stories of their many outings together, their teasing affection contagious, and Rylee found herself laughing along with them.

Coop didn't look amused at Lilly's last comment, however.

"The whisperer thing was a joke," he told Rylee, and turned back to Lilly. "I told you she trained dogs."

"It's all right, Coop," Rylee reassured him. "I've been accused of whispering more than once. The title doesn't bother me."

"It wasn't meant as an insult," he added quietly.

She waved him off. "I don't take it as one. The ability to understand the animals I work with makes me good at what I do."

"Well, I find the whole thing fascinating," Lilly jumped back in. "I'd love to see you in action sometime. Coop says you're a wonder. And your aunt is Silvia Burke, of The Adam's House Foundation?"

Rylee rotated her head and pinned Coop with a raised brow. "Aren't you a Chatty Cathy?"

"Oh, don't be angry with him, honey," Lilly insisted, patting Rylee's arm and drawing her attention away from the adorable flush of crimson flagging his cheekbones. "It's a compliment, really. According to Tim, you're all Coop can talk about these days."

"Lilly," Tim warned beneath his breath, but his mouth contorted into a tight line as if he were trying not to laugh.

"What? It's the truth and I think it's sweet. Besides, a woman appreciates knowing when a man is interested."

"From the look on his face, Coop isn't very appreciative."

Rylee turned, along with both Lilly and Tim, and burst out laughing at Coop's scowl. He shot Tim a steely-eyed promise of reprisal.

"Don't look at me," Tim laughed. "I haven't been able to shut her up since you introduced us."

"Believe me." Coop narrowed his eyes at Lilly. "I've regretted that mental lapse more than once over the years."

"Pfttt…" Lilly blew him a raspberry and tucked an arm through Rylee's. "Come on, honey. I'll introduce you around to some of the ladies." Her voice dropped to a stage whisper as she dragged Rylee away, smirking at both men. "There are a number of ladies here tonight who are dying to meet the woman who managed to get Coop out of the office before nine p.m. not just once, but twice in one week!"

The declaration sent a ripple of happiness through Rylee she shouldn't be feeling. This thing between them had a definite shelf life, and her increasing emotions where Coop was concerned were bound to bite her in the ass when things ended. But knowing he'd been talking about her to his friends and changing his work habits to see her, thrilled her just the same.

Several hours later, the thrill turned to nerves. They bubbled up in her belly as she and Coop exited the cab in front of River View. Tonight was date number three, and while no *official* number existed, she'd heard three was the magic number one needed to reach before having sex with a new man, if they didn't want to be considered a slut in polite society. To tell the truth, Rylee didn't give a damn about the number, or for that matter polite society. After that earlier kiss, she'd gladly take the slut label.

She ached to get her hands on Coop's athletic body, and while the extent of the ache should have scared the crap out of her, just as her increasing emotions did, she told herself not having sex in more years than she cared to count was part of the problem. Probably…possibly…okay, maybe.

So she wasn't tempted with any of the other men she had dated since Marcus to accidentally trip them and rip their clothes off in the process, but that didn't prove anything. Not one of them pressed her buttons the way Coop could with just a look. Cooper Reed brought out her inner slut and she couldn't bring herself to care. Women had needs, just like a man, and faced with a limited number of opportunities to make use of his magnificent body, she couldn't afford to waste any more time.

"I like your friends," she said, crossing the courtyard to her door.

"I like them too," he replied dryly. "Most of the time."

"I liked Lilly especially." She tossed him a grin over her shoulder while sliding the key into the lock. "We're having lunch next week."

"Good God."

She laughed, pushing open the door and entering her condo. He didn't follow and she paused, spinning around. "Would you like to come in?"

Please, say yes. Oh, God, please, say yes!

"Unfortunately, I can't. I have a brief due in the morning."

Stomping her foot in frustration or bawling like a baby would be bad form. Nor could she screech at him like a fishwife, though any of the three were bound to make her feel better. She settled for a grumbled, "I see."

"I have a full docket tomorrow so I won't be able to see you, but I'd like to see you Friday if you're free. Dinner?"

She considered telling him to go to hell and slamming the door in his face. She also considered doing some of that tripping. "Friday is fine."

He leaned toward her and she clenched her teeth against yet another disappointing goodnight kiss. As if changing his mind at the last moment, he straightened and brushed a fingertip over her lips.

"Goodnight, Rylee. Sweet dreams."

The jerk had the gall to whistle as he walked away.

Chapter Nine

"I just don't get guys."

"Food, sports, sex," Brian replied. "What's not to get?"

Rylee perched on the lone stool at the counter of his tiny, galley kitchen, legs crossed, rhythmically slapping an open-backed sandal against the heel of her bouncing foot. Belle lay in the corner while Pippin slurped water from an oversized cereal bowl. Across the room, Brian selected a shirt from the mound of clothes piled on a chair in his studio apartment. He pressed the garment to his nose before tossing it aside to select another.

"I get the food and sports part," she said. "The sex part is where I'm having trouble."

He paused in his sniffing. "It's like riding a bike. You were engaged, Rye Bread. Are you saying you and the mama's boy never went for a spin?"

She narrowed her eyes at the teasing gleam in his baby blues. "I'm not discussing the mama's boy or what he and I did or didn't do together, with you. And I wasn't talking about the rudiments of the act. I was talking about the concept of sexual attraction."

"What about it?" He buried his nose in another shirt.

"Why would a guy kiss the bejeezus out of a woman one minute, then treat her like a...a sister the next?"

His arm dropped to his side and he faced her. "Is that a rhetorical question or a personal inquiry?"

"Personal. I've decided to give Coop a shot."

"I knew it!" He pointed at her, gripping the dangling garment. "Your eyes go all girly when you look at him."

"Shut up," she grumbled. "In case you haven't noticed, I *am* a girl."

"Not to me, you aren't."

She stuck out her tongue and he chuckled.

"As for deciding to give Coop a chance, good for you. It's about time you put the mama's boy behind you." He tossed the shirt aside and bent for another.

"What are you doing?" she demanded.

"I have a date." He straightened, sniffed, and with a nod pulled the shirt over his head to cover his bare chest.

"A date where? At the Laundromat?"

He grinned and crossed the room to the refrigerator. Pulling out two beers, he handed one across the counter. "So, he kissed the bejeezus out of you. Most women would consider that a good thing."

"Bejeezus kisses are a very good thing. The trouble is he hasn't followed up on them." She picked at the label on her bottle with her thumbnail. "I hate when guys give mixed signals."

"What about you?" He sipped his beer. "Women give mixed signals all the time. Maybe he thinks you're not all that interested."

She snorted. "Not possible. I've had my best flirt on, but I must be doing something wrong. Mostly I've just made him laugh." She spoke over Brian's snicker.

"So, help me out here. I don't expect this fling to last. We've already been on three dates, and except for two very promising kisses that ended up going nowhere, I may as well have been out with you."

"Geez, Ry," he furrowed his brow in a pained grimace, "are you asking me for advice on seducing the guy?"

"Well, yeah. What did you think I was asking?"

"I have no idea, but I think you should talk to Sil about this. Helping you figure out how to get a guy into your bed gives me the creeps."

"Sil still doesn't know I've been seeing him, and I'd just assume keep it that way. You're my best friend." She pointed at him with her beer bottle. "*And* a guy. Who better than you to give me pointers? So, what turns *your* crank?"

He choked on his beer. Wiping his chin, he glared at her. "Damn it, Ry. I'm not talking to you about this. Besides, don't all women know this stuff instinctively?"

"My instincts are rusty and you're being a weenie." Cocking her head, she studied him for a moment. "Okay, how about this? Just tell me *one* thing. What is the sexiest thing a woman ever did for you?"

His lips curled in a slow smile and he shook his head. "No way I'm sharing *that*. Besides, unlike you and Coop, the woman and I knew each other for a while, and she was…something of a…"

"Bimbo?" she supplied.

He cleared his throat, but then his eyes glazed over slightly and he grinned. "I'm not sure telling you would help, anyway. I think what she did for me is illegal in New York."

Powerless against his waggling eyebrows, Rylee

laughed. "Okay, skip that. Illegal might be a problem for a lawyer with the D.A.'s office. What is the second sexiest thing?"

He hesitated, but she crossed her arms, refusing to back down. This was important to her, damn it. She was taking a chance, putting herself out there with Coop, and she deserved the reward. She wanted carnal knowledge of the hunky lawyer before things got complicated and she lost her chance. If taking the initiative made her a bimbo, so be it.

"Okay," he said grudgingly. "What are you doing for your next date?"

She shrugged. "He invited me to dinner."

"Make dinner yourself. The old adage about reaching a man through his stomach has some merit. A woman invited me to dinner once and met me at the door wearing…" He paused, his smile widening, but at her questioning glance, he grunted. "Never mind what she was wearing. My point is, guys like when a woman makes a special effort for them. Light some candles and put on some romantic music. Sexy, but not blatantly so. When dinner is ready, use one plate and plant yourself in his lap. That ought to give him the message you're trying to send. If not," he leered, "you can always strip. Only a dead man would miss the significance of that!"

She harrumphed at the stripping comment, but the rest… "Hmmm…dinner at my place. Do you think it will work?"

"Absolutely. Private. Intimate. Add a little wiggle when you climb into his lap. He won't know what hit him."

****

Rylee and Sil crossed the lawn of Lighthouse Park,

the venue for the foundation's first major fundraiser. A half-mile away, River View sat tucked amongst the buildings on the opposite riverbank.

"Guaranteed Elliott is out on the balcony. I can't believe he expected to come along today."

Rylee followed Sil's gaze. Nowhere near the impressive sight of the Manhattan skyline, Long Island City held its own special charm for Rylee. The industrial neighborhood was home, and became home to more and more people every day. Signs of revitalization were beginning to show and her heart warmed to be part of it. Long Island City's industrial face was slowly getting a makeover. With the breathtaking views of Manhattan just across the way, it was surprising the transformation hadn't happened long ago.

She didn't bother squinting to see if Sil was right. The distance was too far. "He's not the kind of guy used to sitting around, Sil. Can you blame him for going stir-crazy?"

"It's been less than two weeks and we're still on our honeymoon. Believe me, I've kept the man busy."

"Eww. I *really* don't want to hear the details."

Her smile sly, Sil snorted. "I wasn't going to share them." She eyed River View in the distance. "Can you imagine him hobbling all this way in that boot? Why, the man is stubborn as a mule."

"Stubborn appears to be a family trait," Rylee complained absently.

Sil slowed her steps and shot Rylee an arched brow. "Oh, really? Since Coop is Elliott's only family, I have to assume you're talking about him. Well, now, isn't that interesting?"

Rylee swallowed a groan and picked up her pace.

"He got you to go out with him, didn't he?" Sil laughed, scrambling to catch up. "I knew that man had potential."

"Don't get all revved up, Sil. We've shared a couple of meals, that's all."

"If sharing a couple of meals is all you're doing, then why haven't you mentioned it?"

"I was trying to avoid this."

"This?"

"Come on, Sil. You practically shoved us at each other during that family dinner. Talk about embarrassing. I'm twenty-eight years old. Long past the age when I need my mommy setting me up with the son of a friend so I won't have to go to the dance alone."

"You have never needed my help attracting boys. Your problem is you let what happened with Marcus keep you from attending those dances. Cooper Reed looks like he'd be light on his feet. I was just helping you see that."

"I'm not interested in dancing. I end up with stomped toes."

"Not when you waltz with the right man." Sil sighed, long and contented. "Then the dance is heavenly."

Rylee grinned, hoping to steer the conversation into safer waters. "I take it Elliott is right at home on the dance floor? Even with the boot?"

"Sugar, that man could introduce a Broadway choreographer to a whole new category of moves."

"The thought of you and Elliott doing the tango should gross me out," Rylee retorted on a laugh. "But I just can't help myself. I'm thrilled to see you so happy."

"I want you to be just as happy."

The gleam in Sil's eyes told Rylee her conversational gambit had run its course, with Sil circling right back around to Coop. Rylee attempted to head her off. "Are we late? I thought we were supposed to meet the administrator at noon."

"She'll be here." Sil waved a hand dismissively. "In the meantime, glossing over things with Coop as just a couple of meals won't work with me. I know you too well. I've been reading you since you showed up on my doorstep, a gorgeous little girl in pigtails with big, wounded eyes." She tucked an arm through Rylee's and squeezed. "I've never told you this, but one of my all-time favorite memories is the day you and I went out and bought that horrendous purple paint you chose when I offered to redecorate your bedroom. Do you remember?"

Rylee blinked, unsure where Sil was going with her sudden change of subject. "I remember. You said the color would give me indigestion, and then helped me look up the word in the dictionary when I didn't know the meaning."

"I fought off a wave of nausea every time I walked into your room." Sil laughed. "But you were pleased as punch with the results. Anyway, I remember standing in that paint department. 'I like this color,' you said and looked up at me, your eyes filled with anticipation of my refusal.

"Oh, Sugar, you have no idea how your eyes broke my heart those first few weeks after you came to live with us. When they weren't flat with despair, they were wide with terror." An edge of suppressed anger sharpened her voice. "You have no idea how many times I wanted to track down your daddy and strangle him with my bare hands."

Rylee grinned at the militant gleam in her eyes. "I've experienced the same impulse on more than one occasion."

"I know you have, but back to my point. After losing your mama, and then going through that circus with your daddy, you'd learned to expect the worst. You expected me to say no that day in the paint department. What's more, since the moment you arrived, scared and lost, you'd been waiting for me to say it was all a mistake. That we weren't going to keep you."

"Sil," Rylee murmured, fighting the sudden sting of loving gratitude prickling the back of her nose and throat.

"When I told the clerk to mix up a gallon of Purple Passion," Sil pressed on, "you looked up at me and I wanted to drop to the floor, right in the middle of that store, and cry like a baby. Your eyes held more than just pleasure at that moment. They were full of wonder and hope for a future you'd already decided would never be yours."

Rylee wasn't sure what to say. Sil's recollection was spot-on. The purchase of that paint marked the first easy breath Rylee had taken in weeks. Terrified, she'd been afraid to hope. She expected a return of her own personal nightmare, constantly waiting for uniformed men and women to appear as they had weeks earlier, when what seemed like most of the New York City police department had invaded her home and ripped her world apart.

They'd secreted her father away in handcuffs, and with no other target for their microphones and cameras, the media turned their feeding frenzy on Rylee. Though the woman from Child Protective Services tried to shield her, the memory of walking the gauntlet to the waiting car still made Rylee break out in a sweat. Her picture was splashed across the covers of the nation's newspapers in the following days, and Sil's description of her eyes at the time was accurate. She'd looked like a hunted animal.

But Sil and Adam changed that, and Rylee didn't understand why Sil brought up the subject now...until she added, "I see the same hopeful wonder in your eyes when you look at Cooper Reed."

"Oh, for heaven's sake, Sil."

"Yes, I know. I'm a dog with a bone. Just don't try to tell me Coop is like those other men you consent to see from time to time because I'm not buying it. Why, the sparks are blinding when the two of you are in the same room."

Denying those sparks to Sil would be a waste of time. The few memories Rylee had of her biological mother were vague impressions of love, a warm smile, a tinkling laugh and a sweet scent. After that day in the paint department, Sil became Rylee's mother in every sense of the word, and her uncanny ability to see inside Rylee's soul was more than a little frustrating at times.

"He's going to hurt me, Sil." She sighed and her arm received another squeeze.

"Of course he will. He's a man, after all. It's what they do."

That made her laugh and helped her shake the heavy mantle her childhood memories always settled on her shoulders.

"But not necessarily in the way you are dreading," Sil added.

"Well," Rylee reasoned wearily. "Since I don't seem to have any willpower where Coop is concerned, we'll just have to wait and see."

"A lack of willpower isn't always a bad thing. I have several pairs of shoes I never would have owned if my willpower was stronger."

"The Jimmy Choos?"

"Mm hmm," Sil hummed with an exaggerated nod.

"God, I love those."

"They're my absolute favorites."

Rylee resumed a quicker pace. "Do me a favor?"

"They're a size six, Rylee. They are *never* going to fit you."

Rylee pinned her with a level stare and Sil heaved a put-upon sigh.

"What's the favor?"

"Butt out on the Coop thing, okay?"

"Oh, sugar…" She grimaced. "Really?"

"Really. The less involved you and Elliott are, the less damage when…" Rylee stopped when Sil pursed her lips in disapproval. "*If* things don't work out between me and Coop. Wave your wand in someone else's direction for now. Focus on Brian for a while."

"The man is a lost cause," Sil complained.

"Admitting defeat?"

Her smile was keen. "Not on your life."

Rylee laughed.

"Ah, there she is." Sil waved at Ada Kelly, the park's administrator, waiting for them at the foot of the large, central fountain. Business hat in place, Sil hurried

Rylee across the lawn.

Over the next twenty minutes, they walked the venue. Clipboard in hand, Ada Kelly described the proposed layout for the booths as well as the placement of the main tent. While Sil and Ada huddled over the plans, discussing the details, Rylee wandered over to the river walk. Securing Lighthouse Park at the tip of Roosevelt Island was a real coup, thanks in no small part to Sil's dogged determination to put Adam's House on the charitable foundations' map. With the courthouse building, the first of Adam's House's successful projects, visible from the park on one side, and the Manhattan skyline on the other, the location was perfect.

Rylee should have been on top of the world. Instead, a persistent echo of trepidation whispered through her head. Maybe her anxiety was due to the trip down memory lane with Sil, or more likely, it was due to the knowledge that her growing fascination with Cooper Reed was bound to leave her in tatters. Either way, today they were finalizing details that would put the foundation on a solid path forward. She should be celebrating, not staring gloomily out at a stunning view on a warm summer day.

"I wish you were here, Adam," she whispered. Her cousin had always known just what to say when the specters of her father's legacy reared up to rattle her. Movement out of the corner of her eye made her turn. Sil stepped to her side. "Sorry," Rylee murmured.

"Why?" Sil kept her eyes on the flowing river. "I wish he were here, too. He'd get a kick out of all of this, you know?"

"More than a kick, I'd say." A smile teased Rylee's

lips. "He'd be running the show."

Sil's sigh ended on a soft laugh. "Adam always did have the tendency to grab the reins of control. He'd be proud of what you're doing here, Rylee."

"What we're all doing. I may have donated the money, but without you and Brian, people would look at Adam's House with nothing but suspicion."

"And they'd be wrong."

Rylee shrugged, jerking her chin toward the panoramic view. "So, what do you think? Will Manhattan's elite be dazzled enough by *that* to open their wallets?"

"Oh, they'll pay up, sugar. If I have to pick their wallets myself."

Chapter Ten

Rylee jumped at the chime of the doorbell. The contrast to the absolute quiet in her condo scraped at her already stretched nerves. "Damn it." She raced across the room to the CD player and pressed the play button. "Calm down, Rylee. Just, calm down."

Three deep breaths almost did the trick. A glance around helped. Sunset painted the sky a brilliant orange, flooding the room with ambient light. Candlelight flickered, the soft and sultry tones of Michael Buble filled the room and dinner smelled awesome. The tangy aroma of her red sauce had bathed her senses when she returned from delivering the dogs upstairs for the evening.

The mirror beside the door reflected the confident eyes of a woman on a mission. A miracle, considering she was shaking in her heels. She ran a hand down the skimpy cocktail dress, resisting the urge to tug at the short hem. Viewed critically, with its miniscule straps, plunging bodice and I-dare-you hem, the siren red dress was an in-your-face statement. Through with waiting for Coop to follow through on those bejeezus kisses, tonight she'd be adding a new ingredient to the mix. Seduction was on the menu.

For days she bounced back and forth between "it's time" and "it's time to run". Decision made, she was pulling out all the stops, starting with this sexy, little red number. If necessary, she would resort to some of that tripping. Cooper Reed would not be leaving the building until she'd had her way with him.

Pasting a bright smile on her face, she opened the door. "Hi."

"Hi, yourself." Coop's lazy blue gaze skimmed from the top of her head to her three-inch heels and back up again. "Nice dress."

"This old thing?"

She grinned when he smiled, and invited him in with a beckoning finger.

"Something smells good," he commented, closing the door.

"I hope you don't mind." She lifted one shoulder in a delicate shrug. "I felt the urge to cook."

"If whatever I smell is half as good as your soup, I'm sure I won't mind at all."

"Would you like a drink?" she asked, moving toward the kitchen.

"What are you having?"

"I have a nice red to go along with the manicotti. It's breathing on the counter, unless you'd like something else."

"That'll do. Shall I pour?"

"Thanks. Glasses are on the top shelf." She pointed to a high, glass-fronted cabinet.

He moved toward the counter, and she stole the opportunity to give him the once-over. The tailored business suit did nothing to disguise the masculine grace of his movements. He reached high to pluck down two glasses, his linebacker shoulders flexing, and she swallowed.

Just when did I become such a rabid shoulder

woman? The hem of his jacket shifted, and she dropped her gaze to the tight curve of male buttock the movement exposed. *And a butt connoisseur?*

He turned to face her, two glasses of dark red wine in hand, and she blinked. A slow smile spread across his face as he held one out to her. She accepted the offered glass and he clinked the rims together.

"To dining in."

The heat in his eyes seared her, and the already erratic thump of her heart kicked into overdrive.

"Mmm," she hummed.

Good call, Brian! I might just be able to pull this off—if I don't have a heart attack in the process.

Hip cocked against the counter, he sipped at the wine and glanced around. "No roommates tonight?"

"They're upstairs visiting grandma and grandpa."

He paused with the glass an inch from his mouth, his smile wry. "I just got a picture of Dad, attempting to bounce Pippin on his knee."

She grinned, pulling the chilled Caesar salad from the fridge.

"I don't know Sil well enough," he continued, "but I can imagine Elliott's reaction to hearing himself referred to as grandpa."

"He likes Pippin."

"One-hundred-sixty pounds of sharp teeth and uncontrollable enthusiasm? What's not to like?" He chuckled at her smirk. "I was referring to the grandpa part."

"Don't you ever plan to have kids?" The question slipped out and she cringed. "Sorry," she said quickly. "Forget I asked."

"Why?" His intent gaze tangled with hers. "It's a

logical question. I haven't given kids a lot of thought. Someday, I guess. What about you?"

"Someday, I guess," she parroted. "Bring the wine, will you?"

She stepped past him, set the salad on the table, and sat down. He followed, taking the seat across from her, and accepted the plate she offered.

"That's the thing about people like us," he said, continuing the dangerous thread of conversation she'd foolishly introduced. "When you're not interested in a relationship, the concept of kids isn't an immediate consideration."

She passed him the covered basket of rolls without comment.

"Was it ever for you?"

"Was what ever what?" she asked, stifling a groan.

"An immediate consideration. Was there ever a man in your life who made you think of white picket fences and the expected two-point-five kids?"

Crap.

Her failed engagement was the last thing she wanted to discuss. The subject would only bring more questions. Maybe she should take Brian's advice and climb into Coop's lap, after all.

"There was a guy once when I was in college," she admitted reluctantly.

"What happened?"

"I was young and he was a dick." She busied her shaking hands by slathering butter over a roll. "We both learned a valuable lesson." She attempted to shove the conversation along in another direction. "What about you? Any potential ex-Mrs. Reeds in your past?"

He smiled. "None."

"Ever been close?"

He shook his head.

"Hmmm…" She cocked her head to study him, breathing a sigh of relief when he didn't immediately pepper her with questions. "What are you, thirty-five?"

"Thirty-six."

"You know." She waggled her fork at him. "When a man reaches his mid-thirties without ever having been seriously tangled with a woman, it means one of two things."

Humor brightened his eyes at her challenging smile. "For the record, I'm heterosexual."

"Phew!" She batted her lashes in exaggerated relief. "For a minute there you had me worried." He chuckled. "From what Lilly says, you have a master's degree in interviewing candidates, but you are still taking your prerequisites in the actual hiring."

"Lilly always did have an interesting way with words."

"Which leaves commitment issues."

"Bingo."

"They say admitting the problem is the first step to recovery."

"If recovery is the goal." The teasing humor faded from his eyes, replaced by guardedness. "I'm content with the status quo."

"Oka-a-ay," she drew out the word. "New subject." She rose from the table and headed for the kitchen, calling over her shoulder, "How about them Yankees?"

He laughed and the subtle tension passed.

"Sil seems pretty excited about the foundation's Fourth of July fundraiser," he said when she returned. "Are you going?"

"Of course." She handed him a plate of manicotti and slid back into her chair. "Are you?"

"I am now."

His eyes were full of seductive promises, his tone deep with the tug of sexual awareness. She stifled a shiver, tempted to sit back and wait, see what he would do next. Maybe he'd just been biding his time, adhering to the mythical third date rule himself.

God, she hoped so, because she sucked at vamping. The minute she opened her mouth, she walked them straight into a philosophical cold shower. Kids and commitments, and white picket fences, for crying out loud! Could she have chosen a topic less likely to whip a man into a sexual frenzy?

But as the meal progressed, though he responded to her clumsy attempts at flirtation, he made no moves of his own. Clearly, if she wanted carnal knowledge of Coop tonight, she would have to be the one to initiate it.

"About the fundraiser," he said, following her into the kitchen and handing her the cloth he'd used to wipe up the remnants of their meal. She flipped off the faucet, leaving the manicotti pan to soak, and faced him. "Do you have any contacts on the inside?" he teased. "I don't seem to have a ticket."

Dinner over, she was no closer to achieving her goal than when he'd arrived. Time to step up the effort.

"I might know someone." She cocked her head, pulling out her best effort at seductive persuasion. Dipping her chin, she peeked at him from below her lowered lashes and pursed her lips in a pout. "But the tickets are hard to come by. What are you willing to pay?"

God, she sounded like an overblown actress in a B

movie.

Humor danced in his eyes and her heart sank. Was he laughing *at* her? Okay, this was ridiculous. Time to try a different tack. She straightened her spine and opened her mouth to ask him flat out why he had yet to take her to bed when he stepped forward, crowding her against the counter. He dipped his head, stopping when his mouth was a breath from hers.

"What did you have in mind?"

Hmmm, maybe she hadn't totally mucked this up. Before she could chicken out, she rested her hands against his lapels, running them up and around the back of his collar. Rising on tiptoe, she brushed her lips against his in a barely-there caress. "Let me think," she whispered.

Fingers tangled in his hair, she pulled his head down. She put all she was into the kiss, opening her mouth to his tongue, thrilled when he accepted her invitation with enthusiasm. His tongue sank deep, warm and flavored with wine, the slight tang of her red sauce and Coop himself. He took charge. As though released from some invisible chain, his arms came around her, yanking her close. The violent shudder of his big body shook her all the way down to her soul.

Hot damn, she crowed silently. *Rylee Pierce, vamp extraordinaire!*

Chapter Eleven

When she melted against him in unspoken surrender, relief crumbled under Coop's need to devour her whole. He accepted what she offered so sweetly, and then demanded more. Tucking her close, he groaned at the way her curves molded to the hard planes of his body. Everything male in him snapped to attention, muscles tightening, blood surging in anticipation of masculine victory. Finally, the waiting was over.

Charmed by her hesitant attempt at seduction, bold one moment, unsure the next, he'd spent the last hour forcing himself to hold back. Instead of swiping the table clean of her delicious meal and spreading her out on the glossy wooden surface, he reminded himself to let her come to her own conclusion on how tonight would end.

But holding back was no longer an option, not with her body plastered to his. The spark of attraction simmering between them from their first meeting burst into a raging inferno and Coop welcomed the lick of flames.

He allowed his need free rein to taste, to touch—to possess. Tongues tangling in a pitched battle of greedy pleasure, his hands discovered the curves that haunted his dreams. His fingers curled around the globes of her ass, sinking into the rounded flesh responsible for that "follow me, big boy" walk of hers. He ground her mound against his erection, his low groan matching hers.

She wiggled her hips beneath the pressure of his hold and the friction shot a flood of white-hot adrenaline straight to his groin. Beads of sweat popped out on his brow. He considered dragging her to the floor, but the desire for the comfort of a bed stopped him.

He gentled their kiss, nibbling at her lips as they continued to reach for his. She suddenly stiffened in his arms and he lifted his head, opening his eyes to find hers squeezed tight.

"Rylee?"

She shook her head.

"Rylee, look at me."

Her lashes fluttered open to reveal eyes black with frustration. She attempted to push out of his arms, but he held her steady.

"Hey, what's wrong? Where are you going?"

"To find a weapon," she ground out. "If you tell me you have a brief you need to work on, I'm going to have to hurt you."

He grinned. "No brief. And I'm not going anywhere, except to find a bed."

"Oh." She blinked. "Good." Her tense shoulders relaxed and she settled in his arms once again. "Because I have to tell you, that habit you have of kissing me senseless and then disappearing is really annoying."

"Not to mention uncomfortable." He flexed his hips to show her the exact location of his discomfort.

"Serves you right," she accused. "You've been

confusing the crap out of me."

He pressed a kiss to the tip of her nose. "I was trying to be a gentleman."

She toyed with the hair at the nape of his neck. "Well, stop. It's irritating."

"Done," he said immediately and she laughed. "About that bed?"

"Follow me."

She turned and he grabbed her hand, but didn't follow. He waited until she paused, glancing back at him over her shoulder.

"Are you sure, Rylee? I don't want you to have any regrets."

She faced him, her smile wry. "I was sure two weeks ago. You're a temptation I can't seem to resist, despite my better judgment," she admitted artlessly. "My brain just needed a little while to catch up with my libido. As for future regrets," she shrugged, "they're unavoidable."

The conversation wasn't going the way he'd expected, but frankly, his body didn't give a damn. She'd just announced she wanted him as badly as he did her, and every male instinct screamed at him to do something about it. But the odd sadness in her eyes made him hesitate. "If you're not ready…"

"Do I look like I'm not ready?"

"You look like every man's dream."

She smiled, rose up on her toes to brush his mouth with hers, and then tugged on his hand as she backed through the condo toward the hallway.

He'd discover the reason for her sadness later. With a wide step forward, he scooped her against him. Her low laughter and slender legs wrapping around his waist tossed fuel on the inferno. One arm beneath her bottom, he went in search of a bed.

"Which way?" he demanded between kisses.

"Turn right." She clung to him, yelping on a laugh when he tumbled with her onto the big four-poster.

The thin straps of her dress fell victim to his haste, but she laughed at the sound of rending cloth while her fingers tore at the knot of his tie. Unable to resist all that gleaming skin, he explored the curve of her shoulder and delicate collarbone with an open mouth. He tugged at the delicate cloth, peeling away the sexy, red temptation to discover she wore no bra, and swallowed with an audible click.

Under her working fingers, he shrugged his shoulders free of both his suit jacket and the shirt she'd unbuttoned, his eyes never leaving the generous mounds of her breasts. Her dusky pink nipples pouted up at him and he lowered his head to capture a peak between his lips. With a growl, he yanked the material from his arms, sending it flying across the room, and then settled down to worship her, as she deserved.

She was exquisite. Her lightly bronzed complexion showed only a faint shadow of the delicate veins beneath her flawless skin. Her nipples, small and puckered, reminded him of the wild berries he'd savored as a boy. They tasted just as sweet, as did the mysterious cleft of her navel. He worked down her body, shedding her of the remains of her dress, peeling away the tiny scrap of lace covering the entrance to paradise.

He brushed his fingertips over the triangle of dark curls and her hips lifted as if to follow the path of his touch. Tempted by the sultry scent filling his nostrils, he dipped his head to feast, but her fingers twining through his hair delayed him. As though her need was as urgent as his, she tugged at the strands, directing him back up her body to fuse her lips to his.

"Coop." Both demand and plea, she whispered his name as her hands skimmed over his chest to his waist. Her fingers fumbled with his belt buckle and he shifted, lifting his hips to discard his slacks with more speed than grace.

"I can't wait to be inside you," he growled, his mouth pressed to the taut tendons of her neck.

"Oh, God." She tossed her head back, giving him better access. "Yes, please," she breathed. Her hands went to his waist. "Let me—ohhh…" She moaned when he delicately bit the curve of her jaw.

He jolted when she snapped the waistband of his underwear. "Another of your briefs," she gasped a heaving breath, "is the cause of one more delay."

A chuckle vibrated in his chest. Rolling to his side, he shoved his shorts down his hips and legs, tossing them aside. He flung an arm over the side of the bed and searched the floor for his slacks and the condoms in the pocket. His muscles quivered with sensual tension, clamoring for that moment when he would slip inside her and find relief. Ripping open the foil disk, he was surprised to find his hands were shaking.

Her eyes were black with passion when he rolled to face her. Like a blowtorch, her heated gaze scorched his naked body, until he was afraid he'd embarrass himself like an untried teenager.

Mounting her, he used his thighs to settle in place, and staring into those dark, "love me, baby" orbs, he reached down to guide himself home, arriving with a single, heavy thrust. She gasped and her eyes went wide, but her legs came around his hips and held him close.

"You okay?" he asked, though his inquiry was a risk. If she called a halt now, he wasn't sure he'd survive.

Her eyes were shaded by lids drooped with sensuality, but humor danced in them as well. "Are you being a gentleman again, Coop?" The question came out on a strangled burst of breath. "I thought we'd settled that."

"Smartass." He swallowed her breathless laugh with his kiss.

He couldn't recall ever having the urge to laugh while buried deep within a woman. Rylee Pierce managed to make him laugh, despite the urge to plunge and plunder clawing at his gut. His shoulders shook with mirth, and with a mental shrug, he accepted that the woman surrounding him with her searing heat was like none other he'd had the pleasure of touching. The realization should concern him, but he'd worry about it later...much, much later.

Past the point of desperation, finesse fell victim to frenzy. His hips surged against hers with ever-increasing speed. The exquisite pleasure of her tight sheath surrounding him drove him toward the abyss. Sweat beaded his skin. Jaw muscles clamped tight, he gritted his teeth against the tingling at the base of his spine, a forerunner to his looming release. A thrust or two would send him hurtling into oblivion and he wanted her with him when he flew.

She moved beneath him, her body gyrating in a dance choreographed by a master. High color stained her sharp cheekbones, announcing she was close. Bending at the waist, he urged her along, gently closing his teeth around a budded nipple. The love bite launched a startled scream from her throat, and with the rhythmic clenching of her inner muscles dragging him, he rocketed over the edge with her.

****

Rylee stared up at the ceiling, her breathing ragged. Coop lay sprawled on top of her, his labored breath huffing in her ear.

It's like riding a bike, Brian had said. Hah! *That* was not like any bike ride she had ever been on, unless she counted her one and only experience on the back of Brian's Harley. She'd staggered away from the hair-raising adventure on legs the consistency of cooked noodles, promising herself never again. With Coop the ride was just as wild, and her body lay spent, like one big noodle, but she was already anxious to climb back on and go for another spin.

Holy cow!

For a guy who left her dangling two weeks, when he finally got down to business, he didn't waste any time. Pouncing on her, he drove her toward climax like a man possessed. He gave her no time to catch her breath, and yet she didn't feel cheated in the least. From the moment he touched her, wave after wave of the most intense pleasure she had ever experienced swamped her, like rising floodwaters pushing her toward ecstasy. Primed and clinging to sanity by sheer force of will, she was surprised she didn't go under the moment he entered her.

Longevity, at least on her part, had *never* been a problem with Marcus. She'd assumed it normal for a woman to fall short of orgasm more often than not, unlike a man. She'd also assumed that when a woman *did* manage to ride the wave to completion, the payoff was a gentle lapping of the tide, fading quickly to pleasant lassitude. How wrong she'd been...on both counts.

With the right incentive, her orgasm was a foregone conclusion, and minutes later her head still spun and her body still throbbed from the powerful whirlpool she experienced in Coop's arms.

The idea of all those *candidate interviews* Coop must have performed to gain his sexual talent made her frown. Still, she couldn't fault the results. And considering the continued, deep bellowing of his lungs, she figured she had some skills of her own.

"Coop," she whispered.

He groaned. "Rylee. Give me a minute, okay?"

She snickered at his gravelly response. "I was just checking to see if you needed oxygen or anything."

His low laugh vibrated through his chest to hers, and with a grunt, he pushed up on his elbows to smile down at her. "Feeling pleased with yourself, are you?"

"You bet your ass." She grinned. "I rocked your world."

"Ah." He cocked his head. "That must have been the rumbling sound I heard...right before you screamed."

When he had a point, he had a point.

"Bet you can't do it again." She laughed when he narrowed his eyes.

Still joined as they were, she couldn't miss his reaction to her sensual challenge. He swelled inside her and her laugh turned into a pleasured gasp.

"I'll take that bet." He lowered his mouth to hers.

"Mmm…" She tightened her arms around him. "I can't lose."

Chapter Twelve

"On three."

Rylee gripped the handle of the sledgehammer with both hands. Above his breathing mask, Brian's eyes twinkled in excitement as he counted down. Beside her Brian's foreman, Tony Camponelli, sent her a wink from eyes full of gleeful anticipation.

Thwack!

The wall shuddered.

"Again."

Thwack.

"One more ought to do it." Brian growled with exertion.

Thwack.

The wall toppled with a satisfying crash and billow of dust.

Rylee lowered the head of the hammer to the floor, fanning the cloud enveloping them. "Oh, yeah. I love smashing things!"

Tony chuckled.

Brian surveyed the results of their destruction. "That's because you have a latent anarchist gene buried beneath your philanthropist's soul."

"That's me. Rylee Pierce, closet rebel."

Brian laughed, propping the sledgehammer against the silent generator several yards away. "Come on, Jamie Dean. Let's get this crap out of here."

The work was dirty and exhausting, and Rylee loved every moment. The foundation and its projects were her babies. If she could, she would've had her hand in every detail, but was smart enough to leave the actual building to the experts. Mindless labor she could do. She fulfilled her need to be involved by never missing the first day of construction. Brian claimed he allowed her to participate in the tear-outs because she was free labor. They both knew he couldn't keep her away, not on day one.

The real construction would begin Monday morning. With the full crew on hand, the place would resemble a beehive. Today, however, she, Brian, and Tony worked in relative peace but for the rock and roll blaring from an old boom box propped on a makeshift table in a far corner.

Rylee gripped the handles of the wheelbarrow, maneuvering the unwieldy load of debris toward the bay doors at the back of the building. A sudden shaft of early morning sunlight snagged her attention, streaming through the opening front door. She dropped the rails of the wheelbarrow to the cement floor with a thump when Coop strolled inside, a tray of coffees in one hand, a baker's box in the other.

"Is this where I check in for duty?" he asked of no one in particular.

The breeze off the river left his black hair mussed and weekend stubble darkened his square chin. Dressed in threadbare jeans and a faded, Harvard T-shirt, molded to the powerful chest she'd explored with her mouth just a few hours earlier, the up-and-coming lawyer looked right at home in the midst of power tools and construction debris.

"Coop." Rylee shot a quick glance at Brian, rolling her eyes at the knowing smile accompanying his raised eyebrows. "What are you doing here? Don't you have a brief you need to finish?"

"I'll get to it later." He looked around the signs of destruction. "I thought you could use an extra pair of hands."

Brian stepped over to the boom box, twisting the dial to lower the volume, while Rylee did her best to hide her dismay.

This morning's session of backbreaking manual labor was meant to serve a dual purpose. First, her need to have a hand in the foundation's latest project, and second, to allow her some time to regroup, analyze her actions and the corresponding emotions of the last few weeks with a clear head.

Because intelligent thought proved impossible with Coop anywhere in the vicinity, she'd left him before the sun came up, asleep in her bed, a circumstance occurring with alarming frequency since the night of her awkward seduction. Not that she minded. On the contrary. This morning she'd had to force herself to walk away from the big, naked, bruiser tangled in her sheets. And therein lay the problem. Being with Cooper Reed was becoming far too necessary for her peace of mind.

Worse, her need to be with him wasn't just for the sex, although, holy cow! She'd never known her body was capable of such sensual greed. Forget slut, she was turning into a nymphomaniac. All Coop had to do was look at her a certain way and the next thing she knew, her panties were down around her ankles. But the quiet conversation, the shared humor and comfortable silences were what worried her. Coop wasn't just another handsome face. He was a nice guy. The type of guy she would happily cast in the role of forever-man— if not for dear old dad.

Just the thought of Pete Morris *should* have been enough to keep her heart in line, but with each passing day, that foolish organ came closer to succumbing to the inevitable. The smart thing to do would be to make up some excuse to walk away, cutting her losses before it was too late.

Unfortunately, with Coop she couldn't seem to manage smart. She was stuck on stupid.

"Coffee is always appreciated." Brian plucked one of the cups from the tray. "So is slave labor. Coop, this is Tony Camponelli, project foreman. Tony, Cooper Reed. He's a lawyer with the district attorney's office." Brian pinned Rylee with a mischievous arch of his brows. "Rylee thinks he's hot."

She gasped and heat flooded her cheeks. The intentional dig earned him a scowl. His answering smile shoved the scowl toward a glare. She had seen that particular smile a thousand times over the years and had come out on the short end of the stick with most of its appearances.

Coop grinned, setting aside the coffee and donuts to shake Tony's hand.

"An extra set of hands will definitely come in handy." Brian ignored the warning daggers she shot at him through narrowed eyes, and indicated her with a nod of his head. "She may look good, but she's too puny to be of any real help."

"Hey!"

"We offered to get her a toy wheelbarrow," Tony

added congenially. "One she can actually handle, but she's stubborn."

Double teamed by a couple of grinning baboons.

Coop eyed her tormentors. "She doesn't look puny to me."

"That's because you've seen her naked."

"Brian!"

"Have you seen her swing a hammer?" he continued, ignoring her horrified outburst. "It's embarrassing."

"You are so dead," she gritted from between clenched teeth.

"Who needs skills with a hammer," Coop's laughing blue gaze scanned her hips, "when you can fill out a tool belt like that?"

Her jaw dropped.

"There is that." Brian grinned, clearly delighted by Coop's contribution to the juvenile razzing.

"Have you seen her walk?" Tony added and whistled through his teeth. "She's a safety hazard in heels. I've banned her from showing up when the crew is around. If I didn't know better, I'd swear she's an OSHA plant."

"Hel-l-o-o-o." She waved a hand in front of Tony's face. "Standing right here. Cataloguing evidence for my sexual harassment lawsuit."

"I can give you the name of a good lawyer," Coop said, deadpan.

The baboons found his comment hilarious.

Three-on-one were insurmountable odds. Especially when the three suffered from a clear case of testosterone overload—left over from junior high, no doubt.

"Morons," she growled, hefting the handles of the wheelbarrow. It wobbled, almost toppling over before she regained control. Male laughter echoed through the building, following her outside.

Five hours later, all evidence of the demolished wall was gone, thanks in no small part to her efforts with the frigging wheelbarrow from hell. Brian had finished marking the windows slated for donation and spray paint striped the floor in preparation of the new plumbing layout.

A layer of dust coated Rylee, including her hair. The guys looked no better. Sweat rings decorated their necklines and armpits. Coop sported a fresh tear in the sleeve of his shirt. They caused a few heads to turn as they shared a beer, and lunch, at the deli around the corner.

Food, sports, and sex, Brian had declared, were the three pillars of modern male interest. The guys covered the first pillar, demolishing their sandwiches, while arguing over the second, debating which team would come out on top this season, the Yankees or the Mets.

"I'm telling you, the bullpen is weak," Brian argued. "They'll fold long before October."

A diehard Mets fan, Tony snorted. "If they do, it's because their payroll isn't the size of the national debt. A salary cap would level the playing field."

Rylee sighed at the familiar dispute.

"You're just jealous because your boys play like bush leaguers compared to the Bronx Bombers," Brian drawled.

"Pussies in pinstripes," Tony corrected and Brian laughed.

To settle the argument, they turned to Coop. He

disappointed them by sitting back in his chair with a smile. "Don't look at me. I'm a Red Sox fan."

Matching groans met his announcement.

"The Yankees are hosting Boston next week." Brian propped his elbows on the table in a clear challenge. "Care to put a little money behind your loyalty?"

"Brian has a connection with box seats," Rylee offered.

"I *used* to have a connection," Brian lamented.

"You broke up with Lucy?"

"Was that her name?" Brian wondered aloud. He grinned at Rylee's disbelieving snort. "Last I heard, she was engaged." His sigh stretched out, long and wistful. "I sure am going to miss…those seats."

Rylee clubbed him on the shoulder. A puff of construction dust floated around his head.

"Damn." He fanned at the cloud. "Tear-outs are filthy work, but we made good progress today."

Tony nodded. "I'm glad you decided on the Cain warehouse, Rylee." Rylee's stomach plummeted and Brian stiffened at her side. Tony went on, oblivious to their distress. "I know you had your eye on the building over on Third. We would have made it work. But this one? This one has style."

Tony jumped, presumably from the toe of Brian's boot connecting with his shin beneath the table. Rylee would have kicked him herself, but for fear she'd hit Coop instead.

The beetling of Coop's brows said he'd noted the implication of Tony's comment. Brian came up with a deflection before she could.

"So, Coop. I hear they've extradited a guy from

Chicago. Word is he's the Queen's arsonist."

"I heard that too." Coop's eyes remained on Rylee, who made a production of wiping down the cap on the catsup bottle with a paper napkin.

"Come on, Coop," Brian pressed. "What's the use of knowing someone inside the D.A.'s office if he won't share details on the biggest story in town?"

Coop finally turned away and Rylee breathed a silent sigh of relief. He'd get back to questioning her on Tony's slip up sooner or later, but at least she'd have some time to come up with a viable explanation for why she would be deciding on foundation sites.

"I wouldn't have much of a career in the D.A.'s office," Coop told Brian, "if I made a habit of sharing the details of an ongoing investigation."

"Well, I'm glad they caught him." Tony shot Rylee an apologetic smile, obviously having realized his mistake. "People were spooked, not knowing where he would hit next."

Disaster averted, at least for the time being, the meal passed in relative peace. As expected, Coop reintroduced the topic on the ride home. Slipping his BMW into the next lane and zipping past a cab picking up a fare, he shot her a quick glance.

"What did he mean?"

"Who?"

"You know who I mean." He kept his focus on the heavy traffic. "You had your eye on a building over on Third, but you chose the Cain warehouse? I thought Silvia ran the foundation."

"Silvia does run the foundation," she said, glad she didn't have to lie. The rest, well, she walked a fine line and didn't like it. "I went to look at the Cain warehouse with Brian because Silvia was unavailable. Elliott came home from the hospital that morning. The day I met you."

"What about the building on Third?" He met her gaze. "Did you look at that the same day?"

His suspicion sliced at her and the death knell on their dating thing echoed like a funeral dirge in her head. She wanted to cry.

"No. I'd seen it a couple of weeks earlier." She sighed. "Look, Coop, Brian is my friend. We do lots of things together. Like the tear-out today."

The subtle accusation in his blue eyes scraped at her conscience like claws. She pivoted her head to stare out at the passing scenery.

"I like him," he said several moments later.

Rylee looked back to study his profile.

"Brian," he elaborated. "I like your friend, Rylee."

Tears stung the back of her eyes and she attempted to blink them away. "I like him too."

His eyes darted in her direction, brows drawn together in a frown. He reached over to cup her chin, lifting her face.

"Hey," he crooned. "What's this?"

"Just tired, I guess."

"Aw, baby." He released her chin and rubbed the backs of his fingers down her cheek. "I'll bet you're tired. I'm beat myself. Go ahead and close your eyes for a bit. I'll take care of you."

For reasons of her own, she took his advice. She slid her eyes shut against his evident concern. Her head dropped back against the supple leather of the headrest, and at that moment, she could honestly say she hated Peter Morris.

Chapter Thirteen

To Coop's way of thinking, there was no better way to greet the day than with an energetic romp in bed with a beautiful woman. Of course, a woman wriggling into a pair of faded jeans wasn't bad either. When the woman doing the wriggling happened to be Rylee Pierce, the exercise was downright erotic.

Coop lay on his back. Head cradled in his hands, he enjoyed the view. The woman had the finest ass he had ever seen. As exciting as the shimmy show was, however, he thought it a shame to cover those luscious curves.

Then again, he couldn't talk her out of her jeans if she were already naked, and getting her naked was an undeniable pleasure. His smartass dog whisperer appreciated the buildup to sex as much as the act itself. He'd never known a woman to take so much pleasure in baiting him until he was mad with lust, then reveling in the results with an appetite that came close to surpassing his own.

Their *dating thing* had stretched to a month. Expecting his interest to wane once he got her into bed, the opposite had happened. The more he had of her, the more he craved.

He'd yet to learn her secrets, and after the tear out at the Cain warehouse last Saturday, he was more determined than ever to discover what caused the sadness in her beautiful eyes. Her explanation when he asked about Tony's comment made sense, but somehow her words didn't ring true. When pressed, she looked almost beaten, as if the effort of explaining fatigued her—a fatigue having nothing to do with the manual labor of the morning.

When they finally wandered down the hall to her bedroom that evening, he expected her to plead exhaustion. She didn't, coming into his arms with sweet abandon and a hungry greed for his touch that made him feel like a king. Physically nothing had changed. She still responded to his every touch with an enthusiasm that never failed to make him go hard. But emotionally she'd begun to withdraw and it pissed him off.

The results of Tim's investigation were due back soon, but what he really wanted was for Rylee to confide in him, tell him what panicked her and made her sad. As the most open, generous and giving woman he'd ever met, he couldn't imagine what she could possibly have in her past that she felt she needed to hide. More importantly, he couldn't fix what he didn't understand, and if they were to have any kind of future, he needed to do just that.

Thinking of Rylee's past in the context of how her secrets would affect his future was a clear indication he was in trouble. Big trouble. He'd told her he wasn't interested in a relationship, but now...

She selected a sleeveless silk blouse from the closet and he rolled to prop himself up on one elbow.

"Come back to bed, Rylee. It's early yet."

Her shoulders stiffened and she slipped into the blouse. "I have an appointment."

"Would you like some company?"

Her head snapped up and he caught the flicker of anxiety she attempted to conceal by spinning around. She made a production of buttoning the blouse while stepping into her heels. "Don't you have to work?"

"I don't have to be at the courthouse until one."

He waited. She didn't answer, moving to scoop up a pair of earrings from the dresser.

"Rylee?"

"Uh, you'd probably be bored."

"If you're not coming back to bed, I'm coming with you." He tossed back the sheet, and rose, naked, to pad to the bathroom of her spacious bedroom suite. "Give me five minutes."

He didn't want to cause her stress, but she would never learn to trust him if he continued to let her push him away. And he couldn't allow her to keep changing the subject whenever he wandered too close to her fears. The time had come to start pushing back.

She'd managed an impossible feat, slipping past his barriers and drifting into his heart like a fine fragrance on a gentle wind. He'd fallen in love with her, but instead of scaring the hell out of him, he found he liked the idea.

His political goals required him to take a wife at some point, but until Rylee, the possibility had left him cold. The institution of marriage had always been a farce in his opinion, and commitment hadn't fared much better. His parents certainly hadn't respected their marriage vows, brushing aside the piece of paper that bound them together without a thought for what their actions would mean to a little boy. As for commitment, his mother hadn't been committed to her son, and although Elliott tried, women and his military career had been his main concern.

Maturity softened the edges of his cynicism somewhat, and witnessing Tim and Lilly Watson's dedication smoothed those edges even more. But Rylee, with her open smile and giving spirit, destroyed his life-long beliefs. Now all he had to do was find a way to make their temporary arrangement permanent.

He meant to marry her.

Instinct urged him to pin her down. To proclaim his feelings, get her to proclaim hers and seal the deal. Experience made him hesitate. Though she clearly enjoyed their time together, she was still skittish. Until he discovered the source of her fear, he would bide his time.

****

"The VA?" Coop pulled the BMW into the Veterans Administration Hospital parking lot. Belle and Pippin were visible in the rear view mirror and he eyed them dubiously. "I'm not sure those two will be allowed inside."

"Not only will they be allowed, they'll be welcomed." Rylee snapped off her seatbelt and climbed out of the car. Opening the back door, she took control of both leashes and directed the dogs across the parking lot. "I'm a licensed Pet Pal handler. This is Pippin's first visit, but Belle is an old hand at cheering up the vets. Aren't you, sweetheart?" She rubbed the Boxer's side. "We visit the boys every Tuesday."

"Pet Pal?" he asked, following her through the front doors.

"A form of emotional therapy," she answered, smiling at the woman behind the front desk. "Watch and learn."

"Rylee!" The gray haired woman shot to her feet to skirt around the desk. "And Belle." Belle greeted the receptionist with her usual grace as the woman smiled up at Coop.

"This is Cooper Reed, Natalie. He's going to help me out today."

"Hello, Cooper." Natalie nodded her greeting then held out her hand, palm down, in front of Pippin's nose. "And who is this handsome boy?"

"This is Pippin. I'm giving him a trial run today to see how he does."

Pippin licked Natalie's hand. When she scratched him between his ears, Pippin's entire body wriggled with pleasure. "Oh, the boys are going to love this one, I'm sure." She straightened. "Do you need me to bring you through or are you okay on your own?"

"We're good."

Passing through the door into the patient's ward, Coop lifted a brow when Rylee handed him Belle's leash.

"What do I do?" he asked, his eyes roaming over the rows of beds.

"Just follow my lead. Belle knows what to do."

The next hour was an eye-opening experience for Coop. The patients in the all-male facility greeted the Boxer like an old friend. For her part, Belle adjusted her approach to each individual patient, propping her front paws on the edge of a bed for an enthusiastic hello or placidly waiting on all fours for the tentative brush of an unsteady hand.

A natural ambassador to conversation, the dog led him from bed to bed, and Coop found himself discussing subjects from the current political climate, to the texture of the tapioca served in the cafeteria down the hall. A military brat, he'd spoken the distinctive armed forces language from the time he could babble. Apparently, he'd retained the ability, for more than one of the men questioned in which branch he'd served. That he was the son of a decorated colonel tempered their disappointment at his answer.

Across the room, Rylee introduce Pippin to the Pet Pal experience while keeping a tight hold on his enthusiasm. As Natalie predicted, he was a hit with the boys. A natural, he seemed to recognize those requiring an extra portion of attention. He showed off his limited bag of tricks then turned his audience's appreciation back upon them, with a wriggling wag of his body and numerous doggy smiles.

Wryly, Coop noted Pippin wasn't the sole object of appreciation for the vets. Smiles widened on bored and fatigued faces the moment Rylee stepped into the room. She charmed the men with her dimpled smiles, easy touches, and teasing laughs. More than one pair of male eyes followed the swing of her hips as she moved about the room.

As though sensing his attention, she met his gaze across the distance. Perched on the foot of a bed occupied by a scarecrow of a man with a grizzled beard, her smile was open, natural. Simple joy shimmered in every line of her slim body.

For a supposedly soft emotion, the punch of love thumping Coop square in the chest staggered him. Her pleasure for the task she performed was obvious from the moment they arrived, and even though her smile wasn't strictly for him, it didn't matter. For a dizzying moment, they were the only two people in the world.

She lifted her hand, beckoning him, and the surreal experience evaporated.

"Herman insisted on meeting you," she said when he approached with Belle.

"So, you're the pirate who's captured our Rylee's eye." Sharp blue eyes studied Coop from a time-weathered face.

"More like she captured mine."

"Can't blame you there, son." Herman nodded. "What's your name?"

"Cooper Reed, sir."

"I knew a sergeant Reed stationed in Germany back in the eighties."

"Could be my father. We were in Germany about that time. He retired two years ago. Colonel Elliott Reed."

"Sounds like him. Semper Fi. Did you follow in his footsteps?"

Coop shot Rylee a raised brow at the unapologetic interrogation. She shrugged and her eyes twinkled with humor.

"No, I didn't, sir. My feet carried me in a different direction."

"Coop is a lawyer with the district attorney's office, Herman," Rylee offered.

Herman's gaze never wavered from Coop. "You have political ambitions, do you?"

Coop chuckled. The grizzled marine may look ancient, but his mind remained sharp as a tack. "I've thought about it."

Coop caught the subtle stiffening of Rylee's shoulders. "You don't like politicians?"

"I don't know any to dislike." She rose and reached into her back pocket. She slipped a packet of teriyaki beef jerky beneath Herman's pillow.

"That's a good girl." Herman patted her hand, and then rubbing Pippin's head, he pinned Coop with a challenging stare. "You treat our girl right, do you hear? I'm still enough of a marine to kick some ass and take names."

Coop nodded soberly, fighting a grin. "I'll keep that in mind, sir."

Chapter Fourteen

"This was a bad idea, guys."

At Rylee's side, Belle sat patiently, while Pippin nosed the canvas bag holding the cold drinks and sandwiches Rylee had prepared. All around them officers of the court came and went in their business suits. Briefcases and Blackberries distinguished them from the civilians who had business at the busy courthouse.

She'd agreed to meet Coop in the park around the corner and should have stuck to the plan. Impatient, she wanted those few extra minutes with him that traveling to the park together would give her. Pitiful and stupid, that's what she was. Since the first time they made love, she greedily grabbed at every possible opportunity to spend time with him, and the results were more than satisfactory.

She never considered herself a particularly sexual person—until she met Coop. In the past month, they'd spent more time in bed than out. Jealousy had never been a problem for her either, but the gorgeous pair of Gucci pumps she discovered in his closet one evening introduced her to the green-eyed monster, and now old green eyes wouldn't leave her alone.

God, she was becoming addicted. She would need a twelve-step program in the end. Stupidly, she couldn't bring herself to care.

However, standing on the courthouse steps in the middle of the busy lunch hour, waiting for a prominent member of the D.A.'s office to join her, was beyond stupid. It was dangerous. Oh, she didn't think anyone would recognize her. Years had passed since the press splashed her image across the evening editions, and she wasn't eleven years old any longer. But she hadn't considered that being seen with Coop might draw unwanted interest in its own right, until now.

The man had political ambitions for heaven's sake. Ponzi Pete's little girl had no business passing time with a man who planned a career subject to public interest—an interest made crystal clear when he descended the courthouse steps. Already a well-known figure in the legal community, many of those swarming the large courtyard hailed him. Stopped for the third time, he exchanged words with a group of suited men, sending her an apologetic smile over one of their shoulders.

Several feet away, a man with an expensive-looking camera followed Coop's gaze. A reporter no doubt, milling about the steps in search of a story. She considered melting across the street and disappearing, but slipping away unnoticed would be near to impossible with two dogs in tow.

She lost her chance to escape when Coop broke away from the group.

Moving down the steps toward her, he smiled. "Am I late?"

He leaned down to greet her with a kiss. She avoided the maneuver, turning on her heel. "No, I was early."

She headed toward the street as quickly as she

could without appearing to run. "It's crazy around here. Are you sure I'm not keeping you from something?"

"I don't have to be back until two." He adjusted his stride to hers. "Are we in a hurry?"

She peeked over her shoulder. Camera Guy stared straight at them. He brought the camera to his eye and she spun back around, increasing her speed.

"Nope, I'm just starved." She jiggled the bag. "I brought lunch."

They reached the curb, forced to stop and wait for the light to change with the others preparing to cross the street. A quick glance back showed Camera Guy closing the distance fast. A muffled groan escaped her lips. If she were alone, she'd take the chance and dodge the oncoming traffic. But Coop would call her crazy and she couldn't endanger the dogs.

"What's wrong?" Coop asked.

She shook her head, willing the light to change.

"Hey." Coop clasped her elbow, forcing her to look at him. "What's going on?"

Nosy photographers were something she should have expected getting involved with Cooper Reed. She'd seen his picture in the paper several times since meeting Elliot, and with plans to run for office at some point, she now understood why the press paid him interest. Any press was good press or so they said, but they were wrong. The wrong kind could destroy lives, and she didn't want to be the noose that hung Coop's political career before it even got started.

Coop wasn't stupid. From his questions, he obviously sensed she was hiding something, and paranoia over a photographer would add to his suspicions. Unfortunately, her evasion couldn't be helped.

"There's a photographer," she nodded behind them. "I think he's following us."

Coop looked over his shoulder. "He's harmless. Just a local society snapper."

The light changed and she charged ahead. Coop kept pace.

"I don't like having my picture taken." She flicked a glance at him to see what he made of her comment.

Humor danced in his eyes. "It's just a camera, Rylee."

"It's an invasion of privacy."

His steps slowed as he glanced back once more.

She tugged at his arm. "Don't slow down, you idiot. He's gaining on us!"

He laughed, but when she sent him a fulminating glare, he sobered. The smile slipped from his face. "You're serious."

"Of course I'm serious." She searched frantically for an avenue of escape. None presented itself. She scanned the sidewalk behind them and yelped. Twenty feet away, Camera Guy continued to close the distance. "Crap, crap, crap!"

"Hold on to the dogs," Coop said and flung up his arm. A cab screeched to a halt in front of them. A moment later, the four of them were jammed into the worn back seat.

"Where to?" the cabbie asked, not at all phased by the over two-hundred pounds of combined dog invading his vehicle.

Coop rattled off the address of his apartment several blocks away, and then settled back in the seat for the short ride. Rylee followed suit, doing her best to calm her racing heart. Considering what had just happened, she couldn't fool herself any longer. It was time she utilized the "walk away as friends" clause they'd negotiated. Instead of the park, they'd be sharing lunch at his place—where they'd inevitably end up in bed. Overall, things couldn't have worked out better, since this was the last time they'd be together.

Coop shoved Pippin away when he attempted a hello kiss, and met her gaze over the bodies of both dogs. "Are you going to tell me what that was about?"

"I thought I had," she answered evasively.

"Did you know that guy?"

"I've never seen him before in my life. I assumed he was following you, Mr. Future District Attorney."

"You're probably right, but I can guarantee he wasn't planning to square *me* up in the viewfinder."

"Are you sure you're a lawyer?" Cocking her head, she studied him. "From the way you managed to ditch him so handily, you have some pretty impressive criminal instincts."

"Rylee." His low tone said he recognized her attempt to throw him off the subject, but he wasn't falling for it.

"I told you." She crossed her arms and looked out the window. "I don't like having my picture taken."

He'd either believe her or not. It hardly mattered. Cooper Reed had to go. And he would. Right after lunch.

****

"Want to grab a beer?" Tim asked from the office doorway.

"Your timing is perfect." Coop closed the file in front of him, pushed the chair back from his desk and stood. He slipped the file into the cabinet behind the desk before grabbing his suit jacket from the back of the chair. Shoving his arms in the sleeves, he straightened the line of the jacket with a sharp tug and grinned. "I thought you had plans tonight. Doesn't being late for dinner with the in-laws qualify as an automatic week on the couch?"

"I know how to get around Lilly," Tim replied.

"So you've said before, but in this case it's not necessary. I'll understand if you need to go."

"Lilly will understand."

At the unexpected seriousness of his reply, Coop studied Tim more closely. The older man's expression grim, he stepped the rest of the way into the office, a file clutched in his beefy hand.

A knot of tension settled in Coop's gut. "What's up?"

He slapped the file against his thigh. "I got the report back on your dog trainer."

He said nothing else, but then he didn't need to. Something red flagged in Tim's investigation of Rylee, and that something was bad enough to make him reluctant to discuss the details here in the office. The knot of tension in Coop's gut grew to the magnitude of a bowling ball.

"Should I skip the beer and go straight to Scotch?" Holding his friend's gaze, Coop waited for Tim to tell him he'd have no need for Dutch courage.

"Probably," he said. "I think I'll join you."

Chapter Fifteen

Coop pounded a fist on his father's door and tried to control his fury. Ponzi Pete's daughter. *Son of a bitch!*

Those flashes of panic, the sarcastic evasions and this afternoon's flight from the paparazzi, suddenly made terrifying sense. As did her cryptic comment when he kissed her goodbye before returning to the courthouse.

"Every woman should have a lover like you, at least once in her life," she'd said.

Her words carried the tone of finality, but at the time he'd been too sated to notice. He'd bet a thousand dollars the brush with the photographer spooked her enough that she'd decided to bolt. Considering her infamous family connection, that worked fine for Coop. But first, he was going to wring her neck!

"Coop!" Sil's smile went wide when she opened the door. Her hand on Pippin's collar kept the dog from leaping on Coop in welcome.

"Where's Rylee," he demanded, not caring when her smile turned to confusion at his brusque tone.

"She's in the kitchen. We—"

He brushed past and his long strides carried him through the condo with Sil and Pippin at his heels. He found her in the kitchen, a mound of peeled potatoes on the counter in front of her. She looked up when he

137

rounded the corner, her quiet smile of greeting fading as he stalked toward her.

Elliott turned at Coop's approach, the boot covering his father's broken foot propped on the rung of the stool he occupied. "Hey, son. What—"

"What the hell kind of game are you playing?" Coop tossed Tim's file on the counter beside the potatoes.

"Excuse me," Sil drawled, but she said no more when Rylee held up a hand.

Pippin whined and she silenced him with a curt command. Belle pressed against Rylee's thigh, watching Coop with intent eyes. Rylee didn't look at the file. She lifted her chin a notch in defense.

"Why don't you tell me what kind of game you *think* I'm playing?"

So pissed he could hardly see straight, Coop propped both hands on the counter, leaning in close. "Alison Rylee Pierce Morris?" he rattled off her legal name.

Her chest expanded with a deep breath but she didn't look away. "You investigated me." Her words were a statement, not a question.

"Damned right I did."

"Coop," Elliott began.

"Hold it, Dad," Coop barked at the interruption. "Do you know who she is?"

"As a matter of fact, I do."

Coop pushed off the counter and spun on him. "And you didn't think her full name was something I should know?" He jerked his gaze back to Rylee. "I've been sleeping with a frigging con artist!" he roared.

The barest flicker of hurt showed in her flinch. She

recovered quickly, but the color leached from her face and her eyes went blank as a doll's. Her usual melodic drawl came out flat and cold. "That's insulting…and untrue."

"Is it?" he mocked. "You've got your hands wrapped around millions of dollars through Adam's House and don't try to deny it. Brian is my friend," he mimicked her southern drawl. "We do lots of things together." He snorted his disdain. "Bullshit! Sil and Brian are your front men."

"You've got it all figured out. Don't you, Mr. Future District Attorney?" She didn't wait for an answer. Swiping up the towel at her elbow to wipe her hands, she turned to Sil. The smile curving her lips didn't reach her eyes. "Would you mind watching the dogs for a little bit?"

Bright spots of color stained Sil's cheeks and her eyes were drenched with angry tears. "You know I don't mind, baby."

Rylee nodded, dropping the towel on the counter before pinning Coop with a cool stare. "You know where to send the police if you decide to file charges for my imaginary crimes."

"Rylee, wait," Elliott pleaded when she skirted the counter. "We need to discuss this calmly."

"There's nothing to discuss."

"Like hell there isn't," Coop snarled.

He reached out, meaning to grab her arm. She jerked to the side and kept walking. Glancing over her shoulder, her eyes resembled chips of black ice. "Then get a subpoena, councilor."

He would have followed when she headed out of the room, but Sil stepped forward, blocking his way.

"Leave her alone," she snapped. "You've done enough damage already."

"*I've* done enough damage," he jeered.

"I cannot believe I defended you, arguing with her when she predicted this would be your reaction if you ever discovered who her daddy is. I'm ashamed of myself for not listening to her. Sorry, Elliott," she said, her furious green eyes never leaving Coop. "But your son is no longer welcome in my home." She reached around Coop to the counter and slapped him in the chest with his file. He scrambled to keep the inside pages from fluttering to the floor.

"Take this garbage with you when you leave."

****

Coop stared blindly at the open file on the coffee table. Beyond the stunning truth of Rylee's parentage, Tim's report contained enough financial discrepancies to catch the eye of a first-year accounting major. Combined with Rylee's hidden involvement in the foundation, no reasonable person could blame him for his assumptions, but he *never* reacted with a knee-jerk response.

He knew all along she had secrets. He should have been better prepared. His only excuse was that love had turned him into an ass.

He'd been fine before he met her. He had a plan. A plan mapped out with careful precision, designed for maximum benefit. There would be a wife one day, an essential component to achieving his political goals. A reasonably attractive woman with whom he could find friendship and mutual respect was all he required. Love hadn't been part of the picture.

Rylee changed that, slipping beneath his usually

reliable radar, destroying all he believed to be true with a simple smile, and he couldn't afford to be wrong about her. Her connection to Ponzi Pete aside, once he'd calmed down, relying on logic instead of emotion, his heart insisted a simple explanation existed for the substantial amount of money unaccounted for in the foundation's financial forms. Adam's House had a track record, one that could be substantiated, of delivering what they promised.

However, unless someone agreed to speak to him, he'd never get that explanation.

Elliott wasn't cooperating. Last night he'd called Coop an idiot right before he slammed the condo door in Cooper's face. But the colonel's belief in Rylee's innocence lessened Coop's concern that he'd let his emotions and her innocent sex persona blind him. The colonel may not have been the world's best dad, but he wasn't a fool.

Brian's reaction was even less cordial. When Rylee didn't answer her door or her cell phone, Coop called her friend to try and track her down. Brian's insulting diatribe proved he'd already spoken to Rylee. He blistered Coop's ear with his suggestion of what Coop could do with his investigation of Rylee and the foundation. The short conversation could have garnered her friend a stint in county lock-up for threatening an officer of the court. Coop didn't bother calling Sil. Rylee's family had circled the wagons. He was on his own.

His gaze zeroed in on the file. He'd been so angry last night, he'd merely glanced at the contents, skimming the front page with its condemning announcement of her birth name. Later, when he'd taken the time to really look, the photographs included in the report were enough to make him sick. They showed a little girl in pigtails, the potential for the beauty she would one day become staring back at him, her eyes filled with a terror no child should ever know. Her eyes held no terror yesterday, but the blank dismissal in them left him chilled.

She'd disappeared, and he needed to find her so they could sit down and talk this through. He eyed the ticket to this evening's fundraiser, sticking out from beneath the remote control on the center of the coffee table. With a cheeky grin, she'd presented the requested ticket one night last week—right before she climbed onto his lap and proceeded to make his eyes roll back in his head, exploring his body with her hands and mouth. The memory was enough to make him break out in a sweat—in fear of never knowing her touch again.

He plucked the ticket from beneath the remote. Tonight's event hadn't been canceled—further evidence of her innocence. If she *were* up to no good, she was too smart to continue as though nothing were wrong, especially now that the D.A.'s office was on her scent. No, like the idiot his father had called him, he'd jumped to the wrong conclusion, and he had his work cut out for him if he was going to repair the damage he'd done.

She would be in attendance tonight, no doubt. Considering how hard she worked at avoiding exposure, she'd be no more interested in a public confrontation than he. Handled correctly, the crowd could be used to his advantage, forcing her to agree to slip away with him so they could speak in private.

The jangle of his cell phone jolted him. Unclipping

the phone from the case at his waist, he checked the name.

"Dad?"

"Brian tells me you're still looking for Rylee," Elliott said without greeting. "Why can't you just leave her be? She can't help who her father is."

"No, she can't, but I deserve some answers, don't you think?"

"For an intelligent man, you can be a real dunce sometimes, Coop."

"She's been lying to me, Dad. You've all been lying by omission since day one."

"That's true." Elliott sighed. "We were trying to avoid this very situation."

"So you just let her string me along, oblivious to the facts?"

"She's not up to anything, Coop. Other than making the lives of returning vets easier. The foundation is exactly what it claims to be."

"Then why all the secrecy?"

"That should be obvious." Simmering anger reverberated in Elliott's clipped tone. "You've gotten to know Rylee over the last couple of weeks and yet your first reaction to learning her true identity was to accuse her of being a thief. What do you suppose the general public, and more importantly, the foundation's contributors would think if they discovered she is Ponzi Pete's daughter?"

His father had a point, but damn it, Coop had been making plans for the future, while she'd been having a fling with a man she didn't trust enough to give her real name.

"Can you blame me for being pissed? Honest

people don't create aliases, and then talk people into giving them millions of dollars." His gaze fell on the file. "I've seen the figures. The foundation is going through cash like a drunken sailor on leave."

"It takes a lot of money to rehab warehouses to make them livable," Elliott argued.

"Except for the most recent one, the buildings were donated. Even factoring in the price of the Cain warehouse, the rehabs wouldn't account for almost thirty million dollars in expenditures."

"No, they wouldn't," Elliott hedged.

"So, where is the money going, if not to an offshore account?"

Elliott didn't answer immediately. When he did, he sounded tired.

"You once asked me how I could afford to buy into River View. The truth is I couldn't, not without scraping together every last penny I have."

"You're broke?" Coop's stomach plummeted. Was it all a fraud, after all?

"No, I'm not broke and that's my point. The foundation, and by that I mean Rylee, subsidized a large chunk of the mortgage, allowing me to buy in at a fraction of the cost. And I'm not the only vet who's gotten that deal."

"Wait a minute. Are you saying she's selling the units below market value?" Coop asked, stunned.

"I'm saying she's charging her vets what *they* can afford, and then picking up the rest of the tab."

Coop's head dropped forward and he stared at the floor. The memory of her smile that day at the VA sliced at him like a serrated knife. He'd seen her affection for the aged and broken warriors, but he hadn't really understood the depth of her commitment to them. Now, he did.

"By the way," Elliott continued, "you know that anonymous, thirty million dollar start-up donation the foundation received?"

"Rylee?" Coop breathed and swallowed back bile.

"Right the first time."

"Jesus." Coop shoved his shaking fingers through his hair. "Why would she do something like that?"

"Sil says she donated the money because she didn't want her father's victims to think she was living off their stolen cash. I say she did it because that's who she is."

Coop's vicious curse echoed in the quiet apartment. "I screwed up big time."

"You don't know the half of it," Elliott replied.

Coop groaned, staring blindly at his empty living room. "What does that mean?"

"Did she ever tell you about her broken engagement?"

"She mentioned a fiancé, said he was a dick."

Elliott chuckled. "That sounds like her."

"What happened?"

"She went away to college, met a young man in med school and fell in love. He asked her to marry him and she said yes. Then she told him about Peter Morris. Two days later, he demanded his ring back and the college administrators suggested she find somewhere else to study. The med student's mother is an important alumnus. Rylee earned her business degree at the community college five miles from Sil's home."

Coop's eyes slid shut. "She's right. He *was* a dick."

"Sounds like a case of the pot calling the kettle

black."

Coop challenged neither the insinuation nor the sarcastic tone. He deserved both. "She must hate me." The possibility settled in his stomach like a brick.

"I doubt it. She should," Elliott added quickly, "but from what Sil says, your reaction is pretty much what she's come to expect when people learn who her father is."

"Speaking of Sil."

Elliott's tone turned downright chilling. "What about her?"

Coop hesitated. As amazing as it seemed, he'd come to believe his father's claims about finding the right woman. Since discovering his love for Rylee, Coop now understood the distinction Elliott had been making that day he'd called to tell Coop he'd married. His father had never been as happy or relaxed as he'd been this past month, until Coop's treatment of Rylee shoved a wedge between wife and son. Torn between the two of them, Elliott's discomfort was palpable. Coop hurt more than just Rylee with his accusations and the thought shamed him.

"Tell her I'm sorry."

The silence stretched out, ending on Elliott's sigh. "She loves Rylee like a daughter, Coop. I'm not sure your apology will do any good."

"Tell her anyway."

"What are you going to do?"

Coop slapped the fundraiser ticket against his knee. "I'm going to track Rylee down and talk to her. Try to make this right."

"Good luck, son. You'll need it."

Chapter Sixteen

Sil worked the crowd at the center of Roosevelt Park. She had promoted tonight's event as a cookout with a sophisticated flair and, from what Rylee could see, she had pulled it off. From the number of guests still milling about the silent auction tables, anxiously submitting last minute bids, the night promised to be a success.

The speeches were over, the slide show presentation detailing the foundation's mission and its accomplishments-to-date completed, and New York's elite were proving they enjoyed a good party. Sparkling cocktail dresses mixed with flip-flops and Bermuda shorts on the open-air dance floor, where wealthy couples did the bump and grind or swayed in each other's arms to the beat of classic rock.

The city's Fourth of July fireworks display would start within the quarter hour and end the night's festivities. With both dogs along, Rylee wanted to minimize the traffic passing by their spot when the guests began strolling toward the river's edge to watch the show. She chose a blanket from among those spread along the shore, settling down several feet from the water, and tightened her grip on Pippin's collar to keep him from wading in.

"Don't look now." Brian wandered over to join them. "The hot lawyer is here and he's headed this way."

He dropped to the blanket and sprawled on his side in front of her. Rylee didn't bother turning around to confirm his claim. After yesterday's vicious accusations, she'd prayed Coop wouldn't make an appearance tonight, but hadn't held out a lot of hope. He'd been trying to reach her and knew she would be here tonight. He obviously believed they still had reason to speak to each other. She didn't.

She kept her focus on the lights of the city across the water, her fingers caressing Pippin's velvety ear where he lay beside her. Belle rested her head on Rylee's thigh.

"Want me to punch him in the nose for you?" Brian asked.

"And deny me the pleasure? No thanks."

"Kill joy," he grumbled good-naturedly.

She smiled.

The clearing of his throat warned her Coop had arrived.

"Rylee," he said behind her. She tightened her arm around Pippin's neck when he started to rise.

"Did you hear that?" she asked Brian. "I thought gnats didn't come out at night in the northeast."

Brian aimed a tight grin in Coop's direction.

Coop stepped around the blanket. "We need to talk, Rylee."

She followed the arching dive of a seafowl, skimming the surface of the river in search of dinner. "Do you have your subpoena?"

"I'm not getting a subpoena, damn it."

"Then I don't see what we have to talk about."

Pippin whined at her side and she looked down.

His confused brown eyes met hers.

I thought we liked him.

That was before.

"We have plenty to talk about," Coop insisted. "Brian, would you mind keeping the dogs while Rylee and I go somewhere a little more private?"

"The dogs and I are fine right here, but if crowds bother you, we'll understand why you have to leave."

"I'm not the one with reason to avoid nosy ears." He lowered his voice. "Ms. Morris."

She jerked her head up to look up at him for the first time. Casually dressed in khaki slacks and a dark blue polo that matched his eyes, the masculine beauty he wore so easily caused a constriction in her chest. The heat of her glare should have had him bursting into flames.

"He has a point, Rylee."

She turned on Brian, ready to blast him. He pointed at the crowd behind her and she glanced around to find he was right. With the fireworks about to start, people were seating themselves at the water's edge. More than one of the event's elite guests eyed them with undisguised interest.

"Maybe the two of you should take off," Brian suggested.

She spun on him. "Whose side are you on?"

"Always yours," he replied quietly.

The understanding in his eyes doused her anger, but not her bitterness. "Then tell *him* to go. I have nothing to say."

"Then I'll do the talking," Coop interjected. "Starting with an apology."

"Apology accepted. Now, go away."

"After I apologize," he went on as though she hadn't spoken. "I think I deserve some answers. Do you really want to have this conversation here?"

"Cooper!"

All three of them turned at the feminine greeting.

"Wow," Brian drawled and sat up. "Friend of yours?" he asked Coop.

Rylee looked over her shoulder and swallowed. A slinky blonde in a painted-on dress of red, white, and blue sequins maneuvered through the maze of blankets in three-inch heels.

"Shit," Coop muttered on a low burst of breath.

If he was after privacy, he failed. The six-foot blonde, decked out in sparkling patriotism, worked the lawn of Roosevelt Park like a Manhattan runway during fashion week. Sophisticated style and rolling hips, she captured the interest of the gathering crowd as she zeroed in on Coop.

Rylee stared at the bedazzled Gucci dreams on the woman's feet and clamped down on the green-eyed monster before it could erupt.

"Ashley. I didn't realize you were here." When the blonde reached his side and lifted her face in expectation of a greeting kiss, Coop brushed his lips over her cheek.

"I'm here with Giovanni." She preened for the crowd, waving an elegant hand in the general direction of the main tent. "He contributed a *gorgeous* off-the-shoulder gown to the silent auction." She skimmed her dramatically slanted blue eyes over Rylee before they landed on Brian. Her predatory smile reminded Rylee of the big cats in the panther habitat at the zoo. "Who are your friends?"

"Rylee Pierce, Brian Hurley," Coop introduced curtly, "this is Ashley Connor."

Brian grinned, all charm and appreciation. "The swim suit edition, right? I knew I'd seen your, ah," he cleared his throat, "face before."

Rylee snorted. Brian ignored her. Ashley didn't. She sent Rylee a questioning gaze. Rylee bared her teeth in an imitation of a smile. "Hi."

"A pleasure," Ashley crooned, but clearly, the introductions held no interest for her. She turned to Coop, her smile bright. "Giovanni was just asking where you were, darling. Why don't we get a glass of wine and go find him before the fireworks begin?" She puckered her lips in a pretty pout and glanced over her shoulder. "You don't mind if I steal Cooper away for a few minutes, do you?"

"I'm in the middle of something, Ash," Coop answered.

Ash? The green-eyed-monster lunged at the bars of its cage. Rylee ground her teeth. Coop's pet names for tall, slinky blondes were not her concern. *The bastard.*

A low growl rumbled in Pippin's throat and he shifted his head to glare up at Rylee.

We don't *like her.*

Rylee tightened her grip on his leash. *No, we don't.*

Ashley pressed against Coop's side, casting a nervous eye toward Pippin. She kept her voice low, but Rylee heard every word.

"Please, darling. It's time we put this misunderstanding between us to rest."

"We broke up, Ash. What's to misunderstand?"

The monster clawed furiously at the lock. Before it managed escape, Rylee rose to her feet. Both dogs scrambled up beside her. "It sounds like the two of you have things to discuss. Coming, Brian?"

Brian hopped up from the blanket.

"Rylee, wait." Coop reached out to grasp her arm, and Pippin, bless his heart, lunged for his favorite lawyer. Rylee yanked on his leash too late. Like a shot, Pippin jumped up. His front paws hit Coop square in the chest with enough force to make him stagger back several steps.

Pressed to Coop's side, Ashley jumped away to avoid one hundred-sixty pounds of enthusiastic dog. Along with dozens of party-goers, Rylee stared, transfixed, as those fabulous Gucci dreams did Giovanni's million-dollar girl in.

Her heels sunk into the mushy ground and her arms pin-wheeled comically. She hit the shallow water at the river's edge with a spectacular splash. Behind her, reflected in the rushing current, red, white and blue rockets raced into the sky to explode in a glittering, patriotic shower. A thunderous boom drowned out her furious shrieks.

****

Wet, frustrated and furious, Coop yanked open the car door. Tim's report, brought along to discuss with Rylee, lay on the passenger seat. With ill-grace he tossed the file onto the driver's seat and bundled Ashley into the BMW with as much gentleness as he could muster. He wanted to strangle her—after he shut her up. She'd been whining, threatening to have Pippin put down and generally bitching since her unexpected dip in the East River.

Thanks to Ashley, with Pippin's help, he'd lost his chance to speak with Rylee. Once assured Ashley was

152

wet, but otherwise fine, Rylee took off with Brian and the dogs. And instead of chasing her down and settling their future, he was dealing with a river-soaked diva he thought he'd left behind weeks ago.

"I've got a blanket in the trunk." He slammed the door before she could lodge any more complaints.

Stomping to the back of the car, he grumbled beneath his breath. When he caught up with that stubborn, dark-haired, dark-eyed witch with the smart mouth and sexy walk, he was going to...

Flipping open the trunk, he retrieved the blanket and stalked to the driver's door. He slid behind the wheel. "Here."

He held out the blanket, but his gaze landed on the file in Ashley's hands. Unease slithered down his spine. Rylee had already been hurt enough because of his stupidity. If the information in the file became public knowledge...

"What are you doing with that, Ashley?"

"Nothing. I didn't think you'd want to sit on it." She shoved it at him in exchange for the blanket. The typical peevishness of her reply helped to allay his concern, but not his frustration.

"Can we go now? I'm freezing!"

Chapter Seventeen

Rylee gasped when the cab pulled to the curb a good twenty yards short of River View's front entrance. After the Pippin-induced fiasco at the fundraiser, she had taken a day to regroup. Flying to Jackson, Mississippi and spending the night in her childhood home hadn't helped. Her life was a mess, and from the look of things it was about to get worse.

"Looks like every network in the city is here." The young cab driver leaned on the steering wheel to gawk at the crowd crammed onto the sidewalk. Mobile TV vans, topped with large satellite dishes tilted like huge, drunken dinner plates, were double-parked on both sides of the street. "Someone famous live in the building?"

More like someone infamous.

"Not that I know of." Rylee fought the cold fingers of dread threatening to cut off her air supply. The memory of another press gauntlet flashed in her mind and she fought back a whimper.

"Th—There's a back entrance." She attempted to steady her shaking voice. "Down the alley. Would you mind dropping me off in back?"

The eyes reflected in the rear view mirror said "get real". "Lady, no way I'm getting my cab through that mob."

"Then take me to…" Her mind drew a blank.

He spun in his seat. "Hey! You ain't gonna puke, are ya?"

She shook her head, opening her mouth to tell him to drive, but she'd waited too long. The first flash blinded her through the window, followed closely by another and then another, until the multiple bursts of light melded into one continuous strobe.

"Damn. Talk about a flash mob!" The cabbie bent over in the seat for a better view.

His comment barely registered over the shouted questions from the jostling crowd rushing the car. Or maybe the buzzing in her ears was responsible for her faulty hearing. But the buzzing didn't drown out the cries of Morris, fraud and Ponzi Pete. Her childhood nightmare had come back to life.

"Please, just drive."

Fascinated fear flashed in the cabbie's rounded eyes. Clearly nervous his cab was about to be crushed, he didn't hesitate. Straightening, he yanked the shifter into gear. "Where to?"

"Anywhere," she said, covering her face with her hands.

****

Rylee sat on the edge of the pink, canopied bed, doing her best to ignore the posters decorating every square inch of the walls. Tony Camponelli's daughter, Suzie, was an avid Disney fan, and Rylee had been right. Cooper Reed's toothy grin beamed at her from the faces of several of Suzie's cartoon princes.

She flopped back on the bed with a groan. Even knowing he wasn't worth the energy, her heart wept at the loss. Before things went horribly wrong at the fundraiser, he made it clear he planned to have it out with her, but she didn't see the point. From the moment she agreed to his tempting proposal, she knew her actions would lead to disaster. Now that they had, she wished he would leave her be.

As with Marcus, the fantasy world she allowed herself to visit for the past month had vanished, exposing the ugly reality beneath. Despite having expected it, her heart bled at the memory of Coop's derision, accusing her of being just like her father across Elliott's kitchen counter.

She had no right wallowing in misery. After all, she'd been there, done that once before, but the razor-sharp fury in Coop's blue eyes had slashed at her until she felt like one of those potatoes she'd been dicing.

She'd been fooling herself, believing her experience with Marcus had taught her the depth of betrayal. But as horrible as that lesson had been, at least Marcus kept his contempt private, sharing it with only Rylee and his mama, of course. In contrast, Coop shared the details of his investigation with the world. The press mob outside her condo couldn't have made his disdain any clearer.

Therein lay the difference between boys and men. Boys were content to run home to mama when their favorite toy lost its appeal, while men were satisfied with nothing less than utter destruction.

The trouble was, although she believed she'd loved her mama's-boy fiancé at the time, she'd since learned the truth. There was no comparing the wispy hold-my-hand-while-we-walk-through-the-park pleasure she'd known with Marcus, to the gripping, touch-me-or-I'm-going-to-die need that had driven her into Coop's arms, despite the expected danger.

With a sigh, she sat up and dialed Sil's number. It would take a lot more than twenty-four hours to purge Cooper Reed from her yearning heart, but his setting the entire New York press corps on her tail should help.

Sil answered on the first ring.

"Rylee!" she gasped. "Baby, don't come home. The press is parked out front."

"I know."

"Then you've heard?"

"I've seen." She breathed deep. "My flight got in about an hour ago. I headed straight home. They pounced on me before I could gather my wits enough to tell the cabbie to leave. They got pictures."

And for the second time in her life, her image would be plastered across the front pages of major news organizations. The first time, she was too young and too traumatized to understand the implications. But things were different now. No longer Ponzi Pete's frightened little girl, she had no choice but to stand her ground. The foundation and its mission were at stake.

"I'm so sorry, Sil. You and Elliott and the rest of the residents don't deserve this."

"Neither do you, so hush. We'll deal with the sharks. Now, what happened? How did they find out?"

Rylee snorted, ignoring the squeezing in her chest. "I think we both know the answer to that."

"Coop swears he didn't tell a soul."

"You spoke to him?"

"Elliott did. He called two hours ago to warn us of what was coming. Apparently, he's gotten a few calls requesting a statement."

Rylee wasn't sure what to make of that. Why would he lie about leaking her identity to the press? The last time she'd seen him, dragging Ashley out of the murky water of the East River, he'd been angry enough to choke someone. Compared to strangulation, blabbing was nothing.

"Do you believe him?"

"I don't know." Sil sighed. "Elliott does, but I just don't know. I know I'm mad enough to wring his neck."

Rylee was surprised to find she could still laugh.

"There's a lot of that going around," she said, echoing one of Brian's favorite phrases.

"Where are you now?"

"I'm at the Camponelli's apartment in Brooklyn. Brian called Tony and Tony's wife, Maddie, insisted I stay with them, at least until I figure out what to do next."

"I just can't believe this is happening," Sil lamented. "I thought we were finally on our way. The fundraiser was such a wonderful success, well, expect for that little incident with Ashley Connor."

Rylee grimaced. "I'm sorry about that, Sil. It wasn't Pippin's fault. I was angry and he took his cue from me."

"Are you kidding? We earned several thousand extra with people hanging around, buying drinks while they chuckled over Ashley's unexpected swim. The extra funds were enough to reimburse her for her ruined outfit, anyway."

Rylee laughed, but sobered quickly. They'd exceeded their goal, with promises of a fresh infusion of cash totaling just under eight hundred thousand. But what would happen to those pledges once the press outside her condo wrote their stories and the articles hit the newsstands?

"I should never have come back here, Sil. I could have hired someone to work with Brian on Agnes's buildings, and you and I could have looked for projects out of Jackson."

"Sweetheart, the two of us were growing old before our times in Jackson. My memories of Adam were killing me, and you were in danger of becoming an eccentric, southern spinster."

"I was born in New York, remember?" Rylee pointed out. "And I don't think I'd make a very good eccentric." She didn't mention spinster, a fate worse than death in Sil's book. Unfortunately, it looked like *A Spinster's Life* would be the title of Rylee's memoirs.

"You're missing my point, Rylee. You did the right thing coming back here, and I'm glad you talked me into coming with you. Why, I never would have met Elliott if you hadn't, and some very deserving families are tickled pink you came back to town."

"Deserving families who will now have the press hounding them, thanks to me."

"Honey, your vets are used to facing enemies a whole lot tougher than the New York press corps. They'll be fine. Now, tell me. What are you going to do?"

"I have no idea, but I'll tell you what I'm *not* doing. I'm not running. Not this time." She scowled across the room at the multiple Prince Charmings. "I haven't done a damned thing wrong."

"That's my girl. Remember, sugar, you're not alone. I'm here for you, and so is Elliott. Brian too, not to mention Tony and the boys."

Sil was right. She wasn't alone. Plenty of people

loved her and believed in her. Peter Morris may have given her life, but she was her own woman, forged under the shadow of deceit and greed. Her record in the charitable world stood on its own merits, and starting tomorrow, she would make sure everyone knew it.

As for Cooper Reed, he could go to hell.

Chapter Eighteen

Rylee's face was everywhere. Several angles of the same shot, her features blurred slightly by the cab's dirty window, graced the front pages of the morning papers. Expecting mug shot quality results from yesterday's flash mob, she was surprised to find that other than the panic in her eyes, the shots weren't so bad.

The articles were something else. Details were slim and facts were even rarer. Innuendo and speculation made up for the lack of information. Several publications quoted the same anonymous source, questioning the connection between The Adam's House Foundation and the daughter of Wall Street's most infamous schemer, Ponzi Pete Morris. In addition, the same source wanted to know why Cooper Reed, the man expected to succeed the city's current district attorney, would help conceal that connection.

If Coop *had* been the one to rat her out to the press, he caught himself in his own trap. His handsome face appeared right beside hers in the morning editions. He'd yet to make a statement, probably because he'd been too busy leaving messages on her cell—thirty-two at last count. One would think he'd get the hint and give up.

Eyeing the crowd on the sidewalk in front of River View, her resolve to set the record straight wavered.

Yesterday's feeding frenzy had shrunk, or maybe the decreased number of journalists had more to do with the fact that the sun had barely begun to rise. A mere handful of determined sharks remained, but the idea of facing even one member of the press made her heart pound with trepidation.

Though she wanted to, she didn't request the cabbie drop her off around back. The foundation's reputation was her main concern, and the sooner she made herself available, proving she had nothing to hide, the sooner the speculation would wane.

Her knees knocked as she climbed from the cab. The half-dozen reporters rushed her before she could take two steps, thrusting microphones and tape recorders in her face.

"Alison Morris?" a cultured voice demanded.

"My birth certificate says Alison Rylee Pierce Morris. I legally changed my name to Rylee Pierce when I turned eighteen."

"Richard Wallis, WCBJ. Why did you change your name? Were you hoping to conceal your identity?"

The model-handsome Wallis had the kind of looks that would carry him straight to an anchor's chair, if that were his ambition. The idiocy of his question qualified him as the perfect candidate in Rylee's opinion. She disliked him on sight.

"Is that a rhetorical question or do you really not know the answer?" The sarcastic remark popped out of her mouth before she could stop. She gulped a bracing breath. "Ponzi Pete Morris is my father." She smiled thinly. "Of course I wanted to conceal my identity."

"So you could follow in his footsteps without notice?"

His green eyes were bright with excitement, as though he were calculating the career boost gained by climbing onto the back of Ponzi Pete's daughter. Rylee didn't understand the appeal of piggyback rides, never had, especially when she was the one expected to do the carrying.

"His footsteps took him to maximum security. If he was your father, would *you* want to follow him?"

Several folks in the crowd chuckled.

"That doesn't answer the question of why you changed your name."

"I changed my name in order to avoid people like you. I faced my first *press conference* the day they dragged my father away in handcuffs. I was eleven." She glanced around pointedly. "It looked a lot like this."

"I don't make the news, Ms. Morris," Wallis pointed out with a lofty tilt of his chin. "I report it."

"Then it must be a slow news day."

"What is your association with The Adam's House Foundation?" someone else asked.

"Adam Burke wasn't just a hero, he was my best friend. I contributed the founding donation to Adam's House, to honor his ultimate sacrifice and the sacrifices of many other brave men and women." She spoke over the multiple follow-up questions. "And before you ask, my maternal grandmother left the money to me in trust. The Justice Department has verified the legitimacy of the inheritance. If any of you are interested, the report is available online."

"So your association is that of a donor?"

"I've been known to swing a hammer on occasion. As a volunteer, I help wherever I can, but I'm not on the board and I don't have access to the foundation's funds."

"You are listed as a resident of River View," Mr. Piggyback pushed. "Adam's House claims to provide housing for military vets. In what branch of the service did you serve, Ms. Morris?"

"Bless your heart," she cooed, bumping up the southern drawl and curling her lips in the sweet smile Sil employed when going in for the kill. "You should demand a rebate on that expensive journalism degree you purchased. They forgot to teach you to verify your facts before you make an accusation. By the way," she added when his handsome face flooded with angry color, "you can call me Ms. *Pierce*."

She turned back to the snickering crowd. "For the record, my grandmother's estate included three warehouses here in Long Island City, two of which I signed over to the foundation as part of my donation. River View wasn't one of them. It's my home."

"Melody Brighton with the Village Ledger, Ms. Pierce." The lone female in the group jumped in. "What can you tell us about Cooper Reed?"

"I can tell you he's gorgeous," Rylee drawled, earning a few more chuckles.

"You'll get no argument from me." Melody grinned before getting back to business. "The two of you have been seen together on several occasions over the past few weeks. What is the nature of your relationship?"

Rylee arched a brow. "I'm a girl, he's a boy."

"You're dating?"

Rylee shrugged and offered the same response she'd given Sil all those weeks ago. "We've shared a few meals."

"What else have you shared?" Wallis interjected.

"Excuse me?"

"He's a law enforcement official and a public figure, Ms. *Pierce*," Wallis clarified. "One who should know better than to become involved with someone with such dubious, familial ties."

"You'll have to excuse me, Richard." She batted her eyelids and cocked her head. "Or is it Dick? I don't share your nuanced language skills. Did you have an actual question or were you making a speech?"

"Did the two of you ever discuss the missing funds from your father's nefarious enterprise?" he demanded.

Clearly, Rylee's back wasn't the only one Wallis planned to exploit. In the scheme of things, Cooper Reed represented the bigger prize. From Coop's wide shoulders, it would be a short climb to the top of the journalism ladder.

The self-important reporter had just handed her the opportunity to deflect attention away from her and the foundation, while gaining a measure of revenge for her battered heart. All she had to do was keep her big mouth shut. The ensuing speculation would be the death of Coop's political dreams.

But her sense of fair play wouldn't let her take advantage of the opportunity. She was as much to blame for her broken heart as Coop. Telling him the truth from the beginning, he would have walked away and none of this would have happened. She gave Coop the cover she wished she could provide for herself.

"Since he knew me only as Rylee Pierce," she answered, "the subject didn't come up."

"And now that your identity has been revealed?"

"Now that it has, we no longer share meals. He's an officer of the law." She bared her teeth in a humorless smile. "And I'm the daughter of a thief. We've moved on."

Melody's disapproving eyes jerked up from her notepad. "He dumped you when he discovered who your father is?"

Pretty much.

But Rylee would be keeping that to herself, and whether Coop realized it or not he owed her a boon. Time to collect.

"His future is bound to include far too many of these impromptu gatherings for my taste." She smirked, satisfaction leaching into her voice. "I dumped *him*."

The reporter's lips twisted in a smile full of feminine approval before rounding in a startled "Oh". As one, the cameras swung to a spot over Rylee's left shoulder.

"Is that a fact?"

Shoulders stiffening, she completed a slow turn to meet Coop's raised brow.

****

"What are you doing here?" Rylee's voice held a bland note of boredom, but Coop wasn't fooled. The wariness in her big, wounded eyes telegraphed her anxiety. At facing him or dealing with the press, he wasn't sure. Being Rylee, she covered her distress with a smartass quip. "Isn't there a deviant jaywalker somewhere you should be investigating?"

Despite the flashing cameras, Coop's grin was genuine. Damn, she was something else. She would make the perfect district attorney's wife. As he'd listened to her, working the press with her typical mix of sarcasm and wit, disbelief warred with respect. Underlying both was relief she hadn't skipped town after all, along with an urgent need to hustle her away, sit her down and coach her through the minefield of media interest—*after* he kissed her senseless.

Though she'd been holding her own with the others, handling their questions with exactly the right lack of concern, she'd made an enemy of Wallis. Coop knew from experience, the network hopeful didn't take kindly to being made the fool. And Rylee managed the feat while the competitor's cameras were rolling. Wallis wouldn't let the hit to his colossal ego go unanswered.

Because of Coop's clumsy handling of Tim's report, the press, led by Wallis, was in full-out attack mode, with both Rylee and he caught in the crosshairs. It would take some fancy footwork to turn the attention to their advantage. Professionally, he'd done what he could to minimize the fallout, officially submitting Tim's investigation to District Attorney Burns. Personally, he still had his work cut out for him. Sizing up the situation, he saw an opportunity to repair the damage with Rylee, while serving up a twist to the story the press wouldn't be able to resist. All he needed was a little bit of luck.

"Now, baby," he crooned. "These people don't know your sense of humor the way I do. They're going to think you don't like me."

To his utter surprise, he witnessed the rare sight of a speechless Rylee Pierce. Her mouth gaped open, but no sound emerged. His grin widened as he enjoyed the novelty of an experience he wasn't bound to face again anytime soon.

Draping an arm across her shoulders, he addressed

the press. "I see you've met my fiancée."

All eyes settled on Rylee, who stilled after her attempt to dislodge his arm had failed.

"I'm not... He's not..." She clenched her jaw and gritted her response to their avid audience. "We are *not* engaged!"

"She's stubborn," he said, winking at Melody. "She won't say yes until she sees the ring."

"I haven't said yes because I was never asked a question," Rylee growled. "He's an idiot," she told the crowd, turning to glare up at him. "You're an idiot."

"The last I knew," Wallis interrupted, "you and Ashley Connor were an item, Mr. Reed. According to my sources, you escorted her home from the foundation's fundraiser two days ago. When exactly did your supposed engagement to Ms. Pierce come about?"

Coop ignored Rylee's accusatory sneer, meeting Wallis' sly smile. Like a murky puzzle finally solved, the scattered pieces shifted into place. Fingers of fury clenched around Coop's stiffened spine.

Tim had spoken to his contacts, attempting to discover who gave the information in his report to the press. Coop never considered he, himself, might have contributed to the leak. The memory of Ashley, holding the file when he brought her the blanket the night of the fundraiser, had been lost in his frantic search for Rylee. And later, after the story broke, he'd been too busy with spin control. He'd only left Ashley alone for a moment, while he went to the trunk, but a moment was long enough for her to have scanned the damning top page.

The smirk on Wallis' face left no doubt *he* had shared the story with his peers, and he'd just named his source. Coop would deal with Ashley later, for now he pinned Wallis with a steely stare.

"I didn't realize you'd been demoted to the gossip desk, Dick. My condolences."

"Something stinks here, Reed." Wallis' cultured tone flattened out in cold accusation. "I'm going to keep digging until I find it."

"If you are truly interested in facts and not just the bitter whispers of an ex-girlfriend, I can help you out."

Wallis bristled, but Coop dismissed him, addressing the others. "About a month ago, I requested an investigation into The Adam's House Foundation and Ms. Pierce. District Attorney Burns released the results of an internal investigation about an hour ago. The report includes the details of my personal association with Ms. Pierce."

Rylee's body jolted under his arm. He tucked her closer and held tight. Several members of the press whipped out cell phones and began dialing, presumably confirming the release of the report.

"You were investigated because of me?" she asked quietly.

He looked down into her eyes, full of horrified concern.

"I volunteered my statement, Rylee. The foundation is on solid ground and so is our relationship. We have nothing to hide."

Her eyebrows beetled. "We don't have a relationship. We *had* a dating thing."

He smiled. "About that dating thing." He dropped his arm from around her shoulders, but maintained a hold on her by wrapping his fingers around her wrist when she tried to move away. With his other hand, he reached in his pocket, pulling out a small black box.

With the tip of his thumbnail, he flipped the top open to reveal a sparkling, square-cut diamond. "What do you say we make it permanent?"

She stared down at his offering, her face shielded from his view by the black curtain of her hair, shining in the muted light of dawn. Her shoulders hitched on a breath, and she looked up at him with tears shimmering in her eyes.

"Haven't you been paying attention to the questions asked here today? You *are* an idiot. What about your political ambitions? My father—"

"I'm not in love with your father, Rylee," he cut in softly. "I'm in love with you."

She blinked at a fresh rush of tears and he held his breath, waiting for her response.

"Um." Melody broke in, her cell phone pressed to her ear. "I *really* don't want to interrupt this, but, according to my notes, The Adam's House Foundation recently purchased the Cain warehouse over on Center Street, right?"

Rylee blinked and nodded.

Melody's eyes were enormous. "I hate to be the one to tell you this, Mr. Reed, but it looks like the D.A.'s office got the wrong man. The Queen's arsonist has struck again."

Chapter Nineteen

Rylee and Brian stood with their arms wrapped around each other's waists, but Rylee wasn't sure who was holding up whom. They'd been on-site more than twenty-four hours, waiting for the okay from the fire department to get back inside the Cain warehouse. Throughout the night, the crowd of onlookers thinned until only he and Rylee remained. The last fire truck had rolled away two minutes ago.

"It could have been worse," she reminded herself, her eyes on the blackened brick exterior of the building.

The place was a mess. Several of the new windows facing the street were broken. The new entry door, installed twelve hours before the fire started, hung from a single hinge. Oily, soot-thickened puddles dotted the walkway and yard.

"God, Brian," she whispered. "What if he had gone after one of the occupied buildings? How could I have born that, knowing I am to blame?"

"Cut it out, Rye Bread." Brian's voice was a harsh echo of his usual low drawl. "I'm too goddamned tired to deal with a bullshit statement like that." When her shoulders hitched and she lost the battle with tears, he looked down at her and groaned. He tightened his arm around her. "Jesus. You're exhausted or you wouldn't be spouting crap. And the Rylee Pierce I know doesn't cry. Where the hell is Coop, anyway? He needs to take you home."

She wasn't too tired to shoot him a teary frown. His weary smile was bright white in his soot-grimed face. Rylee figured she didn't look much better.

Coop had stalked the fire scene yesterday, alternately working the phone and conferring with the arson investigator. Surveying the damage, his blue eyes were hot with fury. When he finally approached her, Rylee listened while he explained his theory of how the press got hold of the story, laying most of the blame at his own feet. He told Rylee of bringing along the file containing Tim's investigation the night of the fundraiser, and leaving Ashley alone with it for a moment or two before taking her home. Frightened and heartsick, Rylee remained silent.

He'd left at dusk, kissing her goodbye before heading back to the office to see to the details of this morning's arraignment of the man responsible for starting the fire. The guilty party wasn't the real Queen's arsonist, or even a copycat as originally suspected, but a sixty-year-old bank manager who had lost everything and never recovered because of Peter Morris.

She scrubbed her cheeks with the heels of her hands, cringing at the slimy goop her tears left behind.

"I'm not saying this is *all* my fault, Brian. Believe me, there's enough blame to go around. But we both know that because of my connection the foundation is a target. It could happen again. I need to step aside."

"The hell you do," Coop said from behind them.

Rylee turned to find him looking tired but clean in a pair of fresh jeans and a short-sleeved T-shirt. He held the leashes of both dogs in one hand. Pippin lifted his large muzzle to sniff at the air while Belle looked around as if surveying the damage.

"It's about damn time," Brian sighed, releasing her with a gentle push in Coop's direction. "Get her out of here, Coop. She's dead on her feet and talking stupid."

Rylee ignored the insult, staring up at Coop. "You have my dogs," she said inanely.

"Possession is nine tenths of the law," he said. "If you want them back, you'll have to give me the right answer to the question I asked you yesterday."

She blinked. Sluggish, it took her a moment to comprehend. "That sounds a lot like blackmail, Councilor."

"My word against yours." He paused, smiling. "Ms. Morris."

She twisted her lips into a smirk, and then raised a questioning brow at Brian.

"I'm frigging exhausted." Brian shoved a hand through his filthy hair. "I didn't hear a thing."

Her jaw dropped open and Coop laughed, brushing his fingertips across her cheek. "I thought you'd appreciate seeing a couple of friendly faces."

"Jerk." She sighed. "You were right. Hello, my babies." She bent to greet both dogs.

Coop stepped close, wrapped an arm around her and pressed a kiss to her hair.

"Don't, Coop. I'm a mess."

"You're beautiful."

"Stop." Brian laughed. "You're going to make me hurl. Congratulations, by the way. Rylee told me you plan to make an honest woman of her. Good luck with that."

Coop chuckled and Rylee rolled her eyes.

"Can we go in now, so I can go home and fall on my face?"

Coop delayed her when she moved toward the building. "In a minute."

"Coop, please. I need to go inside."

"You will, but first, look."

Slipping an arm about her waist, he rotated her until they faced the street. She'd been focused on the building, failing to notice the vehicles arriving at the curb. Dozens of people climbed from cars. Trunks opened, brooms, buckets and boxes appeared. More people came on foot. She recognized some of the faces, residents of both the foundation's buildings. Many others were strangers.

Tony Camponelli led the procession, pushing a wheelbarrow full of cleaning supplies, with Maddie at his side. Behind them, Elliott hobbled beside Sil, using a push broom as a cane. Lilly Watson walked beside Tim, who pushed an industrial-sized vacuum. Rip Cain huffed up the sidewalk toward the building he'd sold the foundation only weeks earlier, wheeling a bright yellow bucket and mop.

"What's going on?" she asked.

"Contrary to what you might think considering the press coverage, there are a few people in this city who believe in you, your vision, and appreciate all you've done."

Like ticket holders to a sporting event they came, swarming the street and sidewalks. With a nod in Rylee's direction, Tony took charge of the small army of volunteers, setting up a makeshift command center and passing out assignments to begin the dirty job of scrubbing away all evidence of the fire. Without a word, Brian wandered over to help.

Rylee shifted in Coop's arms to face him. She could barely speak around the lump in her throat. "You did this?"

"*You* did this." He gently squeezed her. "*I* made a few phone calls."

The tears came again, despite her battle to blink them back. She tucked her head to his chest and held on. With the events of the past twenty-four hours, they had no opportunity to discuss his surprising proposal, but while she had a few things to say about his outrageous method, she couldn't fault his intent. And she wasn't going to let him back out now. For better or worse, Ponzi Pete's little girl had caught herself a man worthy of the name. She'd be keeping him.

"Ms. Pierce?"

Rylee shifted a hand to wipe her tears before turning. A low growl sounded in Pippin's throat and Coop tightened his hold on the leash.

Melody Brighton stood several feet away, a half-dozen willowy beauties surrounding her. Rylee's eyebrows arched. Dressed more appropriately for a society luncheon than a post fire mop-up, their presence drew the attention of more than one pair of male eyes.

"Ashley."

Coop's voice held a note of warning and Rylee groaned when her gaze settled on the tall blonde at the center of the group. The last forty-eight hours had been hell. She was too tired and grimy to clash verbal swords with a stunningly beautiful, vindictive bitch right now. Relieved when Ashley addressed Coop instead of her, the blonde's words caught her by surprise.

"My friends and I are here to help, Cooper, and I'm

also here to apologize." Her hesitant blue gaze dropped to Pippin before swinging to Rylee. "I acted badly, Ms. Pierce. Cooper's obvious interest in you stung my pride. I acted without thinking. But this." She lifted a graceful hand to indicate the destruction. "This is just ugly, and I'm sorry for my part in causing it. Forgive me."

"I guess I could do that." Rylee shot a sidelong glance up at Coop and smiled. "Since I can see myself lashing out under similar circumstances."

A smile curved the lips of Giovanni's million-dollar girl.

"But, Ashley?" Rylee added.

"Yes?"

"If you ever come near Coop again," she said sweetly, "you won't have to worry about my dog. I'll kick your ass myself."

Coop threw back his head on a bark of laughter, and Melody and the lovelies surrounding Ashley joined him. Pippin added to the melee with deep-throated barking. The joyous sound, in the midst of so much loss, lifted some of the heaviness from Rylee's shoulders.

"I'll keep that in mind." Ashley kept a wary eye on Pippin, but her smile remained. "Come on, ladies. We've got work to do."

"They'll be more of a hindrance than help." Melody followed their progress as they strolled over to the command center. "But the pictures will make great copy."

"So, you're here in an official capacity?" Rylee asked the young journalist.

"I'm always a reporter, but I'm here because I

agree with Ms. Connor. This entire situation was ugly from the start. If you'll let me, I'd like to help you set the record straight. Beginning with that proposal I interrupted yesterday." She glanced at Rylee's left hand. "I don't see a ring."

"He's stubborn," Rylee said, repeating Coop's words from the day before. "He won't give me the ring until he hears my answer." She grinned at Coop's mock scowl.

"Well?" Melody prompted.

"Yeah, well?" Coop added.

Rylee held out her left hand, wiggling her blackened fingers. Juggling the leashes, Coop pulled the box from his pocket but didn't immediately slip the ring on her finger. With her hand in his, he hesitated, his eyes full of love and promise.

"Don't you have something to say to me first?" he asked.

"Yep."

"Then go ahead."

"I'm really glad you suggested that dating thing."

"Me too." His eyes narrowed in warning. "What else?"

She looked down at the dogs, meeting Pippin's excited eyes.

He's my boy! The one you said would love me as much as I love him.

A startled laugh bubbled up her throat and she jerked her gaze back to Coop. "Pippin thinks you'll make a fine daddy."

A wince crossed Coop's face and he swore. "Are you sure that condition isn't negotiable?"

"I'm sure," she said and grinned.

He dodged the tongue Pippin swiped at their joined hands, but humor twinkled in his eyes. "Fine. And?"

"And I'm not sure I'll make a good political wife."

"I am." He leaned in until his mouth brushed hers. "Say it, Rylee."

"I love you, too, Cooper Reed."

Rylee didn't give a thought to the flash of Melody's camera. She paid no heed to the picture they made—the handsome young attorney, his mouth lowered to that of the grimy philanthropist with a heart for heroes and troublesome dogs. But the resulting photograph earned a cherished place in her heart, and introduced the world to America's future attorney general and his dog-whisperer wife.

A word about the author...

Mac is a wife, mother, really young grandmother and breast cancer survivor living her dream. Along with her husband of thirty years, a neurotic Pomeranian, and a blind cat, she lives in Phoenix because the southwest feeds her soul.

Thank you for purchasing
this publication of The Wild Rose Press, Inc.
For other wonderful stories of romance,
please visit our on-line bookstore at
www.thewildrosepress.com.

For questions or more information
contact us at
info@thewildrosepress.com.

The Wild Rose Press, Inc.
www.thewildrosepress.com

To visit with authors of
The Wild Rose Press, Inc.
join our yahoo loop at
http://groups.yahoo.com/group/thewildrosepress/